T

UNITED STATES OF BILLIONAIRES BOOK 7

LENA SKYE

Fancy A FREE Romance Book?

Join the "**Romance Recommended**" Mailing list today and gain access to an exclusive **FREE** classic Romance book along with many others more to come. You will also be kept up to date on the best book deals in the future on the hottest new Romances.

* Get FREE Romance Books For Your Kindle & Other Cool giveaways

* Discover Exclusive Deals & Discounts Before Anyone Else!

* Be The FIRST To Know about Hot New Releases From Your Favorite Authors

Click The Link Below To Access This Now!

Oh Yes! Sign Me Up To Romance Recommended For FREE!

Already subscribed?
OK, Read On!

Summary
"A Story of sex, money and..... mojitos."

Young student Nina Wilson just wanted to have a bit of fun in Miami. But she ended up getting much more than she bargained for.

When she met local billionaire Alex Conrad she immediately fell head over heels for a man who wasn't just wealthy. He was kind, charming and extremely driven too.

He was perfect.

And when Nina discovered she was pregnant with his child it felt like a dream come true.

However, there were a lot of things about Alex that Nina had no idea about.

And very soon the truth about how Alex made his first billion would be a truth that would come back to haunt both of them....

This is a steamy billionaire romance with elements of mystery and suspense. Only read this if you want an addictive page turner that will have you absorbed till the very end!

Copyright Notice
The Billionaire From Miami © 2018, Lena Skye
ALL RIGHTS RESERVED.
This book contains material protected under International and Federal Copyright Laws and Treaties. Any unauthorized reprint

or use of this material is prohibited. No part of this book may be reproduced or transmitted in any form or by any means, electronic or mechanical, including photocopying, recording, or by any information storage and retrieval system without express written permission from the author / publisher.

Contents

Chapter1
Chapter2
Chapter3
Chapter4
Chapter5
Chapter6
Chapter7
chapter 8
chapter 9
chapter 10
chapter 11
chapter 12
chapter 13
chapter 14

Chapter 1

Spring Break

"Come on, Nina. I know you didn't just come here to hang out at the beach. Let's live a little. It's our last night in Miami. Let's party it up."

Nina sighed, pulling her sunglasses down and looking her best friend in the eye.

"Jasmine, I thought we agreed we would stick with the beach, hang out at some college parties, and stay away from downtown clubs. I don't want to end up hungover and lost in the city. What if I miss my plane? I have midterms next week."

"That's crap," Jasmine said, rolling her eyes. "I don't know why they're doing that to us."

Nina shrugged.

"Studies showed that people tested better after a break, not before. It's science, deal with it."

Nina laughed and leaned back in her beach chair, staring at the waves and inhaling the smell of the salty air.

"You're so uptight. You were never like this in high school."

"Yeah, but I want to get a job and have a future. We're about to graduate in May. We can't afford to screw this up now. We're almost done."

"So, that's it? You're just going to spend the rest of your life being a boring, uptight accountant?"

"That's the plan."

"Nina, *come on.* We're in Miami. The clubs stay open twenty-four seven. The weekend starts on Monday here, damnit. If we've ever been in a better place to party and let loose for just one night, please, tell me now."

"When have you ever needed the perfect location to party?"

"You know what I mean. And frat parties are different. This is you and me. My ride or die. Our last hurrah before we graduate and have to adult it for the rest of our lives. I'll fly the straight and narrow tomorrow. I'm asking for one night."

"*And* you asked me for one vacation. Here we are. Jasmine, you promised me that you wouldn't push it. I didn't want to come on spring break in the first place. I have so much to do, and I can't afford to get less than an A on my—"

"Just stop it, Nina. You could skip your midterms and still graduate in the top ten percent. You have perfect grades. It's not going to hurt you to get tuned up. Just this once. Please? For me? When we graduate, you know we're not going to see each other much."

"That's not true, Jazzy. We'll see each other as much as we can."

"Of course, we will. At first. And then, our monthly, meet-in-the-middle get togethers will turn into once every few months, and pretty soon, I'll forget when the last time I saw you was."

"Can you cut the theatrics?"

"Can you live a little?"

Jasmine stood there, hands on her hips, face set. Nina knew that expression, and she knew that Jasmine wasn't going to let it go. They'd been friends for a decade now, and Nina knew she wasn't going to win this fight. Jasmine would wear her down until she finally gave in. She sighed again, wishing that her friend was a little more cautious. They weren't teenagers anymore.

"Fine," Nina said.

Jasmine squealed in delight.

"You won't regret it, Nina."

"I'm already regretting it. We need to set some ground rules, 'cause I don't want to end up stranded again."

"That happened one time."

"One time is too many. What's the plan if we get separated?"

"Meet back at the hotel?"

"I don't like it."

"Worst-case scenario. It's not going to happen."

"I'm already wishing I'd said no."

"You're going to have fun, Nina. I promise."

"Where have I heard that before?" She started gathering her things, packing them into her beach bag and taking one last look at the pristine shoreline. "The sun is setting soon, so we might as well go back to the hotel and get ready."

"You're right, just one more thing."

"What?"

"Promise me that you're not going to half-ass it tonight. Have fun and live a little. You have the rest of your life to lead a boring, careful existence."

"Some of us like predictability."

"I'm not saying that your life can't be predictable. But this is spring break. It's practically like Vegas."

"What happens here, stays here?" Nina said wryly.

"Exactly. Just don't get on that plane tomorrow and wished you'd danced with a cute guy or shared a kiss with no expectations. Or more."

"I'm not gonna—"

"It's one night. Nina. It's not going to be this life-changing mistake you're afraid it's going to be.

It's just one night of fun before we head out to the real world."

Jasmine was staring at her, waiting for her to agree. When Nina finally shook her head, Jasmine hugged her roughly.

"You're right," Nina finally conceded. "It's just one night."

***

Pulsing music met them on the street as they exited their Uber, stepping onto the sidewalk. They followed the crowd walking through the front doors of the Fontainebleau Hotel.

"This place is huge," Nina said. "Maybe we should find someplace a little smaller."

"Are you kidding? LIV is the most exclusive nightclub in downtown Miami. What are you worried about?"

"Nothing," Nina lied. "You don't think my skirt is too short, do you?"

"Stop stalling, you look sexy."

Jasmine reached out, undoing another button on the tight blue shirt Nina was wearing, exposing more of her cleavage.

"That's a little much, Jasmine."

She reached up to rebutton the shirt, but Jasmine slapped her hand out of the way and shook her head.

"It's just right. Try not to be so rigid. Let loose for once in your life. Promise me you'll have fun."

Jasmine stuck out her pinkie finger, a silly throwback to their middle school days. Nina rolled her eyes, then laughed, taking Jasmine's finger with hers and swearing that she would have a good time.

"Alright, let's get this party started."

The bouncers opened the heavy double doors, and the music overwhelmed them, its rhythmic, thumping beat driving the scores of college kids already on the dance floor. Nina followed Jasmine through the crowd, making their way to the bar. Before Nina could say anything, Jasmine ordered their drinks, and handed her something pink with sprinkles on the rim.

"I don't want to be hung over," Nina shouted, but Jasmine shook her head to indicate that she couldn't hear, shoving the drink into her hand and taking a sip of her own.

Jasmine closed her eyes and licked her lips, savoring the first sip, then gulping down the rest and leaving the glass on the bar. Nina sighed, taking a taste, then throwing the rest back and putting the glass down beside Jasmine's. It was delicious, reminding

Nina of the birthday cake ice cream she'd left in her freezer back home.

Nope, she thought, *not going to waste the night.*

She'd made a promise to Jasmine that she would live it up and have a good time, but more importantly, she'd made a promise to herself. This time tomorrow, she would be studying for her first midterm exam, and in just over two months, she would be a college grad. Jasmine was right; life was about to get really boring and really predictable. It was time to live it up and have fun.

"You're smiling," Jasmine said, shouting to be heard.

Nina nodded, the familiar warmth of a good drink flowing through her. Already feeling lighter, she danced into the crowd, moving her body to the music and laughing with Jasmine. In no time at all, everything faded away except the crush of bodies surrounding her on the dance floor.

She felt hands on her hips, and a man slide up against her, but she didn't care. She was having fun, and he was a good dancer. She turned around, smiling into dark green eyes and putting her hands on his shoulders while he moved effortlessly with her.

He leaned close, and for a second, Nina panicked, thinking that he was going to kiss her neck. But when he spoke into her ear, she relaxed.

"You're a good dancer," he said. "I've been watching you."

"From where?" she asked, one arm around him as they moved around the floor.

"From the VIP balcony. You want to join me?"

"No. I'm here with my friend."

"The girl in the yellow dress?"

"Yeah, how did you—"

"She ducked out with a guy a few minutes ago."

"What?"

Nina looked around, shocked to see that he was right. Jasmine was nowhere to be seen. She thought back, trying to remember when the last time she'd seen her friend and realized it was a while ago.

"I have to find her," Nina said, stopping to pull out her cell phone.

She scrunched up her face when she saw that she had a missed text from Jasmine.

Catch you at the hotel, it read, with no other explanation. Nina scowled.

"Is everything alright?"

"Yeah."

She put her phone back into the small purse she wore across her body, getting back into step with him, even though she was frustrated with Jasmine. Not surprised, but frustrated. They were supposed to be on this trip together, and now she was on the dance floor alone.

"I can help you look for her, if you want," the man offered, but Nina shook her head.

"No. I'll see her at the hotel."

He smiled, flashing his perfect teeth and stepping forward to take her in his arms to dance once more.

What the hell, she thought. Jasmine had left her there to hook up with some guy. She was already here, so she might as well enjoy herself. Besides, the man smelled delicious, and he had a beautiful smile. She decided then and there that she wasn't going to worry about what Jasmine was doing, or who. She was going to enjoy her night, starting with letting go of her inhibitions and making sure that she didn't leave Miami regretting being too uptight.

Nina smiled up at the man, getting in closer so that their bodies slid against each other while they danced. He pulled her in closer, following her cues without question. He was incredibly handsome, with sandy blond hair, and a natural tan that said he spent plenty of time outdoors. His shoulders were broad, and she'd bet anything that the body beneath his clothes was just as strong and chiseled as the rest of him.

He leaned down again, and this time, she was sure he might kiss her. She tensed, anticipating the moment, then shuddering when his breath tickled her ear as he leaned in to speak to her again.

"Are you okay?"

"Yeah," Nina said. "It's just so loud."

"Come with me," he said, taking her hand and leading her off the dance floor.

She followed, not sure where they were going, then deciding that she didn't care. The crowd parted in front of them as they went, and she realized that they were following a big, beefy man in a crisp suit with an earpiece in his ear.

"Who's that?" she asked, still following her dance partner.

"That's Jaime," he said without elaborating.

Jaime opened the door for them, holding it as they exited, his head constantly on swivel.

I wonder why he needs a bodyguard, she thought.

He led her down a long corridor to an elevator, stopping in front of it and smiling at her.

"Where are my manners? I'm Alex. Alex Conrad."

He waited a beat, reached out and tucked a strand of her straight hair behind her ear. She watched his lips, mesmerized by him. Then she blinked, laughing at herself.

"I'm sorry, what did you say?"

"I asked your name," he repeated, completely unbothered by her momentary lapse.

"Nina. Nina Wilson."

"You're not from around here, are you?"

"How did you know?"

"The sweet Southern accent was my first clue."

"What was your second?"

"You don't strike me as the typical party girl."

The elevator opened, and Jaime checked it before standing in front of the sensor and waiting patiently. The door tried to close on him, but he ignored it.

"Would you like to come up to my suite?"

"I'm not sure," she said.

"No pressure. You just seem like the kind of woman who would prefer a private pool and a gorgeous view of the ocean more than a loud, sweaty nightclub."

He was right about that.

"Maybe just for a little while," she said.

Alex smiled.

"Perfect."

He held out his hand to her and she took it, letting him lead her into the elevator. Jaime positioned himself in front of the doors, using a key to select their floor.

"Do you take your pit bull everywhere you go?" Nina asked.

"Jaime? No. He'll sweep the room, then he'll wait outside."

She was waiting for him to elaborate, but he didn't. Instead, he rubbed his thumb across her knuckles, his hand still holding hers. He caught her staring at his fingers. Slowly, he brought her hand to his mouth, brushing his lips over her skin so gently that a shudder passed through her.

She licked her lips, taking in a deep breath as her nipples hardened in response to him. He was oozing sensuality, and she found her thoughts straying to dark places. Alex didn't move, holding her gaze as she inhaled the scent of him and struggled with her self-control.

What was it about him that made her want to throw caution to the wind and kiss him right there?

The bell on the elevator sounded and the door opened, granting her a moment of reprieve.

Jaime led the way, opening the door and doing a quick walk-through before exiting again just as quickly. As the door clicked shut, she realized that she was completely alone with Alex in a spacious living area.

The east wall was entirely made up of windows, offering a beautiful view of the ocean in the light of the full moon. There was a huge balcony with a private pool and a jacuzzi. He led her onto the balcony, standing beside her while she took everything in.

The warm breeze caressed her skin, as soothing as the sound of the ocean below.

"This is amazing," she said, shocked by the luxury surrounding her.

"It has five bedrooms and two levels. Would you like to take a swim with me?"

"I don't have a suit."

"Neither do I."

His intention was clear, his voice pitched low. A chill shot through her body.

His hands were already on his shirt, pulling it over his head and revealing the smooth, tanned skin beneath. She wondered for an instant if he had tan lines, but he removed all doubt when he removed the rest of his clothes.

"You must spend a lot of time sunbathing here," she said, taking in every line of his perfect body.

"I don't live here. I live in Coconut Grove."

"That's just across the bay."

"I know." He smiled. "I'm spending the weekend here trying out my newest buy."

"You bought the penthouse?"

He laughed, then shook his head, reaching out and working open one button on her shirt at a time.

"No. I bought the hotel and the nightclub."

Nina stared at him, shocked by what he'd said.

"The *entire* hotel?"

He was still working on her buttons, taking his time as they spoke.

"Yes."

"Wow."

He smiled, brushing the back of his knuckles against her skin.

"Being rich has its perks," he said. "The night is young. Let me spoil you."

"I leave for Lexington tomorrow."

"University of Kentucky?"

"Yes."

"What time is your flight?"

"Two."

"I'll have you there by then."

"I have to meet Jasmine at the hotel before then."

"Send her a text."

"I have to pack my things."

"I'll have someone pack your things and bring Jasmine and your things to the airport."

"Is there any issue I can find that you can't fix?"

"No."

She sighed, looking into his deep green eyes.

"Give me one night, and I'll show you a world you've only dreamed of."

"I can't miss my flight; I have midterms tomorrow."

"You'll be there with time to spare."

"I really shouldn't stay."

"But you want to."

"I do."

He leaned in, one hand still cupping her cheek, his lips capturing hers with aching tenderness. As soon as their lips touched, she knew without a doubt that she was going to spend the night with him. No man had ever made her feel the way he had with just a simple kiss.

She almost wished that she wasn't leaving Miami the next day.

Chapter 2

"Can you swim, Nina?"

"Of course, I can swim."

"Good," he said, pushing her shirt off her shoulders and revealing her blue, lacy bra. He rubbed his thumb over the soft swell of her breast. "I love how this color looks against your skin. You're beautiful. Like fine chocolate."

His finger slipped beneath the strap of her bra and she held her breath, waiting for him to slide it down.

He was watching her, and with a wicked smile, he left her strap where it was, his large hands trailing down her ribcage and over her hips. He slid her stretchy, curve-hugging skirt down in one smooth motion, and letting it fall in a puddle of fabric around her feet.

"Have you ever been skinny dipping before?"

"No," she said.

"There's a first time for everything."

Hands on her waist again, he pushed her lacy panties down as she stepped out of her shoes. Hands slowly working their way up, he released the clasp of her bra with one hand, then cupped her breasts in his hands.

"You're even more beautiful naked."

"So are you."

He drank in the sight of her, stepping back so he could get a better view in the soft lights on the balcony. Her body trembled, her excitement mounting, but he held out his hand to her instead.

"First, we swim. Then, I'll have my way with you."

It was a promise she was certain he was going to make good on.

He led her into the private pool, pulling her into his arms and floating around the pool with her. He kissed her again, this time more deeply. She slid against him in the cool water, wrapping her arms around his neck and holding him close.

He moaned into her mouth, responding to her when she deepened the kiss and held him tighter. Pushing against him, she teased his rigid erection with her body, hoping that he would lose control and take her right there in the pool.

He pulled away, smiling at her.

"I have plans for you," he said. "And I don't mean in the pool."

"What kind of plans?" she asked, heart racing in excitement.

"Patience. We have all night."

He scooped her up in his arms, cradling her against his chest and holding her there in one strong arm. With his free hand, he explored every curve and swell of her body, his movements unhurried.

Her body was on fire, his touch driving her mad, but Alex wouldn't be hurried. Clearly, he was enjoying himself.

"Have you seen the ocean at night?" he asked.

"Not like this."

"I want to show you why I love this city."

Still holding her in his arms, he walked up the steps and out of the pool. She wound her arms around his neck, leaning against him as he carried her.

"There's nothing like the wind on bare, wet skin," she said.

"There's nothing like a naked, beautiful woman in your arms," he countered, his voice low and thick with need.

He walked onto the part of the balcony that faced east, setting her down by the railing. She put her hand on the smooth bar, leaning against the glass and looking out onto the ocean. The moon had risen completely, shining brilliantly across the dark waters.

Alex stood behind her, his hands around her waist, holding her against him. She could feel his excitement, and her own anticipation grew in response. She wiggled her ass against him slightly, drawing a warm chuckle from him.

He slid his hands down her arms, then covered her hands with his on the railing. When he moved against her, she arched her back, offering herself to him silently.

He kissed her neck, still holding her hands on the railing as she stared across the ocean. When he slid into her, she rose up on her toes and arched her back even more, her breath catching in her throat as her body stretched around him.

"You're so wet," he whispered, nibbling her ear and moving inside her.

The wind swirled around them and the waves crashed below, heightening her excitement. Her breath was coming in quick gasps and a fire was growing between her legs. She gave herself over completely, and when she finally came, it was the strongest orgasm of her life.

She was pinned between him and the railing, the tips of her toes barely touching the deck as he rode her hard. She cried out, wave after wave of powerful orgasms rocking her body. When Alex finally joined her, the tension was already building within her again, sending her spiraling into oblivion and igniting a fresh wave of orgasms in the process.

Leaning against him when he thrust into her for the final time, she listened to his heart beneath her ear, his hot skin against her cheek, his strong arms holding them both against the balcony.

He was still inside her, and he was still hard.

There was a light chiming sound, and with a groan, Alex slid from inside her, grabbing a towel from a nearby lounge and wrapping it around his waist.

"Stay there," he said. "I'll be right back."

She did as he asked, looking out at the gorgeous view and thinking about how amazing the week had been. Spending the night with a rich man was the perfect end to a perfect week, even if that wasn't what she'd intended to do.

She turned when she heard him come back out the sliding glass door, going to him when he reached out his hand.

"Who was that?"

"Room service. I ordered dessert."

Taking her into the spacious master bedroom, he sat on the bed and patted the seat next to him. A decorative tray sat on the bed, half a dozen large, chocolate dipped strawberries on the tray.

Alex took one, feeding it to her before he took a bite of his own.

"This is delicious."

"I thought you would like dessert."

"You thought of everything," she said, taking a second strawberry when he offered it and savoring every bite.

"You have no idea."

"So, why a hotel with a nightclub in it? Have you always wanted to own a hotel?"

"I like to invest in a diverse mix of real estate. I have several different types of properties. This is my third luxury hotel, but my first with a nightclub in it. I love Miami, and I love the nightlife here. I wanted to own a little piece of that."

"I'd hardly call it little. And what about this suite; is it always going to be reserved for you?"

"No. I'm in the business to make money. I have a home, and it's beautiful."

"I'm sure it's lovely."

"Nowhere near as beautiful as you are."

She smiled, ducking her head slightly. Now that she'd had her needs taken care of, she was feeling a little less feisty, and his attention caused a warmth to flood through her that she'd never felt before. Men didn't usually have this effect on her, but Alex Conrad wasn't like most men.

When he fed her the last strawberry, he set the tray aside and reached out to her. But she slid off the bed instead of going to him, holding out her hand and arching an eyebrow playfully.

"Want to go for round two?"

"You sure?"

"I am, but this time, it's lady's choice."

"Intriguing," he teased.

She turned, taking his hand and leading him back out to the balcony to one of the larger lounges that was more like a lounging bed than a chair. It was padded with a soft fabric, a built-in pillow running along one side of it. She pushed him down, then straddled him. She rubbed herself against him, hands on his shoulders, stroking him until he was hard against her sex.

Reaching down, she took his hands and put them on her breasts, then she slid onto him, taking him inside her. His hands were rough, squeezing as she rocked on his erection. This time, she came fast, her excited flesh already prepared for him.

Her nails dug into his shoulders and when he pinched her nipples roughly, she laughed.

"That feels good," she said, arching her back and riding him hard.

When the orgasm hit her, she pressed her hips into his, dragging every last drop of pleasure from him before collapsing onto his chest in a heap. She was breathing hard, her skin damp beneath his hands.

They lay there like that for a long while, wrapped in each other's arms on the heavily padded lounge on the balcony. Before she knew it, she was drifting off to sleep, though she knew she should get up and at least attempt to make it to the bed.

"It's so nice right here."

"We can stay here, like this," he said. "Let the sunrise wake us up."

"That sounds perfect," she mumbled.

She heard him chuckle and felt his lips on her head when he kissed her tenderly. His arms were around her, the gentle breeze off the ocean the perfect temperature. She could already feel the darkness creeping in, and she let herself relax into him. Naked, outside on a balcony in a luxury suite in a strange city, Nina had never felt more right. Tomorrow, she would have to go back to her old life. But for right now, everything was perfect.

Chapter 3

"Girl, where have you been?" Jasmine said when Nina got to the security line at the airport. "You barely made it."

"But I made it, right?" Nina teased.

"Yeah. Here's your boarding pass. Good thing you got here, because I was about to give up and just go through security without you. The line is ridiculous."

"Where's our stuff?"

"They checked it at curbside. Courtesy of the man who brought me here in a Bentley. Nina, what in the world happened last night?"

"You ditched me to hook up with some guy." She paused for effect. "Again. And I met someone."

"And you spent the night with him? Who the hell is he? He's obviously loaded."

"I did. And he is. Loaded."

Jasmine was smiling from ear to ear.

"I'm going to need all the details."

"Not right now. I just want to get through this ridiculous line and get on the plane. Once we're on the plane, I'll tell you what went down."

The security agent took their boarding passes, scanning them with a handheld device and checking their IDs.

"You'll go to that line. The one marked first class," the woman said.

"First class?" Nina said.

"That's what I said," the woman repeated shortly. "You have first class tickets, so you go through that line."

Nina was about to question the woman again, but Jasmine grabbed her arm and pulled her toward the much shorter line.

"What's going on?"

"I don't know. When tall, dark, and silent checked our luggage in, he printed off our boarding passes for us. It took him forever, but I wasn't about to complain. When he handed them to me, I thought they looked different, but I thought maybe the paper at the airports were all different."

"I guess Alex upgraded it for us."

"I'm not mad." Jasmine laughed. "If he wants to throw his money our way, let him."

"I had the best time with him," Nina said wistfully. "I wish we didn't have to leave today."

"See? You shoulda gone clubbing with me earlier. I knew if you'd just chill and let yourself have a good time, you would enjoy it. Now, you're regretting missed opportunities. Who knows, you coulda been Mrs. Rich Dude by the end of the week if you'd rode that a little longer."

"Whatever," Nina said, laughing at Jasmine doing a little dance as they moved through the line.

When they made it to the front, a second agent led them to the screening area, but when they went to remove their shoes, the man waved dismissively.

"Leave them on. Just pass through the scanner."

They did as he asked, whizzing through security in record time.

"Maybe you should sleep with rich guys more often." Jasmine laughed.

"It was something."

"What happened?"

"We slept on the private balcony and woke up with the sun. Then, we had breakfast in bed, watched a movie on a giant screen that appeared out of a table, and we swam some more, then we had sex one last time. Then I came here."

"Did he drive you here?"

"No, he had a meeting or something. We said our goodbyes at the hotel."

"I bet you did."

"You're so ridic."

"I told you, you'd have a great time if you just took that stick out of your ass. Where did you get that outfit? It's gorgeous."

Nina looked down at her neat, powder blue slacks and perfectly cut, white button up shirt beneath the smart little cropped jacket that matched the slacks. The outfit was elegant, but understated, and she planned on wearing it to every interview she had. She felt like a million bucks, and the matching pumps were icing on the cake.

"They appeared, just like everything else. Being rich is pretty fantastic, or at least, it seems that way."

"I'm impressed."

"You should be."

"I'm serious. You took a chance and you had a great time."

"And now, it's back to real life, and now the real work starts. The rich may have it easy, but the rest of us have to make a living."

"Oh, but for one night, everything was perfect, wasn't it?"

Nina smiled, Alex's handsome face still burned into her memory.

"It's a night I know I'll remember for the rest of my life."

They got to the gate just as they were boarding first class seats. Nina and Jasmine slid into line, presenting their boarding passes and following the group to the front of the plane through a heavy curtain.

"This is nice," Jasmine said, sitting in the large seat beside Nina. "I didn't realize how packed into those seats we were. You could easily fit thirty coach seats in this area, but there are only twelve seats."

"Let's not make it obvious that we're not used to first class."

"You're right." Jasmine laughed.

Nina shook her head, still laughing at her friend. She settled in, staring out the window and replaying the night over and over in her head as they waited for the rest of the plane to load.

His hands on her breasts. His face when he looked at her. Waking up in his arms on the balcony, still naked. Wearing his shirt while he cooked breakfast in the huge kitchen in just a pair of pajama pants. She hadn't expected him to cook, even though the five-bedroom, five-bathroom suite included a gourmet, fully stocked, kitchen. Somehow, the fact that he could afford to have everything handed to him, yet he still knew how to make the perfect omelet, made him even sexier.

"Did you say his name was Alex Conrad?" Jasmine asked, interrupting her thoughts.

"I did."

"Nina. Do you know who he is?"

"The owner of the hotel and the nightclub. He told me."

"Not just that. Nina, he's not just rich. He's the richest bachelor in Miami."

"Okay. That doesn't really change anything. I knew he was rich."

"He's more than rich. He's a freaking billionaire."

"That still doesn't change anything. We had one great night, but that's all it was. He didn't make any promises, and I didn't make any plans to come back. You hook up with guys all the time and never see them again. What's the big deal?"

"I don't hook up with billionaires who treat me like a spoiled princess. If I did, that would be my last hookup."

"You're a hot mess."

"Miss Nina Wilson?" a flight attendant asked, interrupting their conversation.

"That's me."

"This was sent for you."

He handed Nina a gift bag, leaving before she could ask who it was from.

"I hope it's an engagement ring," Jasmine said, only half-joking.

"Stop. You're being ridiculous."

"Are you going to open it?"

"I am."

Inside the gift bag was a small box wrapped in elegant black paper, wrapped with white ribbon and sealed with a wax heart.

"Fancy," Jasmine said. "What's zChocolat?"

"I guess it's chocolate."

Carefully, she unwrapped it, revealing a beautiful, wooden box with a gold emblem on the front in the shape of an old-fashioned skeleton key with a heart-shaped top.

"I've never seen chocolate that came in a wooden box before. There's a card, what does it say?"

Nina pulled the card out of the box, revealing a dozen golden hearts. Nina read the outside of the card and furrowed her brow.

"Edible 24-carat gold?" she read out loud.

Opening the card, she couldn't help but smile at the message within.

Nina,

I had a wonderful time last night. If you're ever in Miami again, I'd love to take you out on a proper date, maybe show you more of the city. I hope you enjoy these chocolates. They're dark and silky; the most delicious I've ever tasted. They remind me of you. Safe travels.

Always,

Alex Conrad

His phone number was written on the bottom of the card.

Nina took one of the hearts out, carefully placing it in her mouth and biting down. To her surprise, the gold didn't feel like metal. The first taste of the impossibly perfect chocolate hit her tongue then, and she closed her eyes and moaned softly.

"Are they that good?"

"Have one. But just one."

Jasmine laughed.

"It must be good if you don't want to share."

"It's amazing."

Jasmine took a heart from the box, putting it in her mouth.

"Damn, this is good."

Nina closed the box, holding it on her lap and letting the last bite of chocolate melt in her mouth. The flight attendant got on the intercom, going over the same safety lecture they'd heard a thousand times as the plane pushed away from the gate.

But Nina wasn't listening. She was looking out the window, thinking about the man who did sweet things like upgrading their tickets to first class and sending a five-hundred-dollar box of chocolates to the plane before it took off. He's more than made good on his promise to spoil her, and Nina couldn't let go of the twinge of sadness over leaving.

Alex was everything she'd ever fantasized about, but they lived in two different worlds, and it wasn't like she could just jump off the plane and run to him. That only worked in the movies. In Nina's world, men made big promises that they rarely kept, and dating was more about getting her in bed than getting to know her. She was living in a fantasy if she thought that Alex loved her after one night together.

She would cherish the memories, but that's all their night together would ever be; a sweet memory.

The plane was speeding up now, then, they were in the air, speeding away from Miami and leaving spring break behind. In a few months, Nina and Jasmine would graduate from college, and then there would be no fairytales, and no jetting off to spring break for a last hurrah before they entered the workforce. She was closing a chapter in her life and making way for the woman she knew she would become. There was no room for fantasy in that life.

Sighing heavily, she leaned back in the large, comfortable chair and stretched her legs out all the way without touching the chair in front of her. She was determined to enjoy this last bit of luxury before they landed in Lexington. She would savor the chocolates until they ran out, and then she would put away the box and the card, and she would move on with her life. And Alex Conrad would fade away until he was nothing but a distant memory.

Chapter 4

Two months later

"I wish you'd stop pacing, Nina."

"I'm just nervous. My stomach is in knots."

"Nina, you've got this. You worked your ass off to graduate summa cum laude. You deserve this."

"Thank you. And I did. I just didn't know that it would mean giving a speech."

"I thought you're giving the speech because of your overall GPA. Lots of people graduated at the top of their class, but there can only be one number one, and that's you. Breathe. Relax. You're going to make yourself sick."

"I feel sick. I'm nauseous and I have the worst headache. Maybe I just shouldn't give a speech. They have a backup, you know."

"Summer?" Jasmine sneered. "I can't believe you just said that. No. There's no way I'm going to let you let that arrogant twat have the moment that *you* earned. We all know that she paid people to write all her papers. She skated through half her classes while you worked your ass off."

"You're right, I did."

"And Summer obviously bombed her finals, since she doesn't do her own work. It's a great combination."

"She did," Nina said, smiling. "But, it didn't matter. The only way she could have beat me is if *I* failed *all* my finals. She didn't have a chance even though she's a dirty cheat."

"I bet she's furious."

"She's out of control, but she's hiding it well. Her father made another large donation to the school during spring break. She thought that would buy her something."

"Yeah, a free education."

"She won't say anything, but I could tell she was upset when she found out. It's silly. She's got the second highest GPA."

"Second place is first loser."

"I think that's exactly what she's thinking."

"She's lucky no one can prove that she paid someone else to do her work."

"That's one of the downfalls of the internet. They'll never be able to prove it, at least not quietly. If they launch a full-scale investigation, dear old daddy will find out and he'll stop donating to the school. They won't risk that; that's what she's counting on."

"I can't wait to see her face when you're up there."

"What about you? How did you do?"

"They don't give out an award for 'just barely graduated' so I'll be enjoying your speech from the alphabetized section of the graduates."

"Ouch."

"A degree is a degree. I doubt anyone is going to care about my transcripts as long as I graduate."

"You're probably right."

Nina's stomach churned, and she took a deep breath, putting her hand to her stomach and frowning.

"Did you take something?"

"No. I'm fine. As soon as I get on the stage, I'll be fine."

"Just focus on me, alright. Now, let's get going. It's almost time for the commencement and we still need to take pictures. We're never going to see some of these people again, and I want some pictures for my dartboard."

Nina laughed.

"You don't have a dartboard."

"I don't, but it made you laugh, right?"

"It did."

They left on foot, dressed in their cap and gowns, ready to face the future head-on.

"I was thinking about taking another vacation before we have to start working."

"I can't, Jazzy. I have interviews lined up every day next week."

"Already?"

"My scholarship money runs out at the end of the month. I'll have to find a place to live, and I can't do that until I know my budget. I can't know my budget without knowing what my salary is."

I thought you saved all the stipends that came with your scholarships."

"I did, but that money isn't going to last forever. I need to pay a deposit, turn on utilities, and—"

Nina stopped, reaching out and grabbing Jasmine's arm to steady herself.

"What's wrong?"

"I just feel awful."

"Maybe you're coming down with something."

"I hope not. I can't afford it right now."

"Do you need to sit down?"

"No. I've got this. Can we just slow down?"

"Sure," Jasmine said, putting an arm around Nina and slowing her pace. "Just relax. We're in no hurry."

"Thanks. You're a good friend."

"I'm the best friend."

"And so freaking humble." Nina laughed, though her voice was softer when she did.

She took a deep breath with each step, trying to calm her nerves so she could make it through commencement. It would be over soon, and all she had to do was get up there and give a short speech. Then, she could relax.

"Better?"

"A little bit."

"It's almost over."

They walked up the steps into the huge auditorium, and Nina found her chair, waiting patiently while the seating filled up and the commencement began.

Her hands were shaking when the dean finally nodded her way, letting her know that she was the next speaker. She quietly made her way to the stairs, walking onto the stage once her name and academic accomplishments were announced.

The applause died down, and she found Jasmine in the crowd. Her friend gave her a thumbs-up, and Nina started her speech.

She took her time, careful to breathe slowly and evenly. She felt awful, but she was able to push through it, and in the blink of an eye, it was over, and she was heading toward the stairs again.

Her head felt light as she took the first step, then she felt as if she was floating. She heard a collective gasp from the crowd, but she was struggling to figure out what was going on, and how she'd ended up in a crumpled heap at the bottom of the stairs when she was still holding the rail.

"Nina!" Jasmine yelled, pushing through the people that had already gathered around her.

She knelt behind her, putting Nina's head on her knees and taking the wet handkerchief that appeared out of nowhere. There was too much going on around her, but when the cloth touched her head, Nina closed her eyes and the ruckus started to fade.

"I think I'm sick," Nina mumbled.

"It's alright. The paramedics are on their way."

Nina tried to shake her head "no," but the motion made her gag.

"I don't need paramedics," she whispered.

"I know. Just close your eyes and relax. Jazzy's got you."

Nina didn't respond. She was so tired, and it felt so good to just rest.

She felt hands on her, then a cool, firm mattress beneath her. Her body rocked as they wheeled her out the side door, and only her empty stomach saved her from retching.

"Nina, my name is Sara. Nina, you're going to feel a little prick, then cold, okay?"

"That's what she said," Nina muttered.

Jasmine laughed from the jump seat on the other side of the ambulance, her hand wrapped around Nina's.

"Jokes are a good sign," Sara said. "We'll get you to the hospital and they'll get you sorted out. I'm giving you some D-50. Your blood sugar is really low. Have you eaten anything today?"

"She didn't feel good when she woke up," Jasmine offered. "She skipped breakfast."

"Got it. This should help her feel better pretty quickly."

Nina listened to the two of them go over her morning, the paramedic gathering as much information as she could on the short ride to the hospital. Nina was already starting to feel a little better, though she was still more exhausted than she'd ever been in her life.

"How are you feeling now, Nina?"

"I understand what my grandma meant by 'bone tired' now."

"Have you been sick?"

"Not really. I've been feeling off for a couple days, but I woke up feeling horrible this morning."

"Have you been around anyone that has been sick recently?"

"No. I've been studying."

"We're here now. We're going to get you in the ER and turn you over to the doctors, okay?"

"Thank you, Sara."

"No problem." Sara and her partner pushed the gurney out of the ambulance and toward the doors. "You get to feeling better."

And just like that, they'd passed her off, leaving her in the care of the emergency room doctors.

There was a flurry of activity, with nurses filing in one at a time, drawing blood, asking her questions, and telling her they'd be back ASAP. Then, they were all gone, and Nina was alone in the small room with Jasmine.

"Are you feeling better? You look better."

"I do. I think I'm coming down with something, though."

"Better now than the first week of work, right?"

"It is. But I have an interview first thing Tuesday morning. I hope I'm better by then."

"That's in three days."

"Don't remind me."

She groaned, leaning back and closing her eyes.

When Jasmine shook her a few seconds later, she opened her eyes and looked around. The doctor was standing there, a soft smile on her face.

"I must have dozed off," Nina said apologetically.

"You need to stock up on sleep now."

"Am I sick?"

"Not exactly, but I did have them put Zofran in your IV, and I'll send you home with a prescription. How do you feel?"

"A *lot* better. Still tired, but the nausea is gone."

"Good. When you leave here, you'll want to make an appointment with your OBGYN, and you're going to need to make sure you don't skip meals anymore."

"My OBGYN? I don't have one. Why do I need one?"

The doctor looked surprised.

"Have you noticed any changes in your body, besides the nausea?"

"Yes, but I thought that was just because I've been under a lot of stress lately."

The doctor looked at Jasmine, and Jasmine shifted uncomfortably.

"What's going on?" Nina demanded.

"I'm sorry," the doctor began. "Usually women are at least aware, and I thought you'd already gotten a positive test at home."

"Positive for what?"

Even as she asked the question, she knew. Her heart sank, and she began to panic. This couldn't be happening, not now. She had plans and goals, and she needed a job and a place to live off campus. The timing was all wrong.

She waited, hoping that the doctor wouldn't confirm her worst fear. She needed to hear it from the doctor.

"Well, we did a blood test, and you're pregnant. According to your numbers and your LMP listed on the intake form, you should be right around eight to ten weeks. Your doctor can confirm."

"I don't have a regular doctor. I just go to the campus doctor. I'm never sick. Are you sure that I'm pregnant?"

"I can have them do an ultrasound right now, if you want."

"Please. Maybe it's a fluke."

The doctor smiled, disappeared for a few moments, then returned with a machine on wheels with a square, old-fashioned screen.

Nina sucked in a quick breath as the cold gel hit her skin, then she held her breath as the doctor searched, then smiled.

"There they are," she said, hitting a few buttons and printing off a small picture. "It looks like you're due around Christmas, give or take."

"When would I have conceived?" she asked, but she already knew.

Her hectic academic life didn't leave much room for relationships. She couldn't remember the last time she had sex before Alex, but she knew that it had been long enough. Unless she was about to give birth in the next few days, it was Alex Conrad's child.

"Around the last two weeks of March. You're eight weeks along."

"Spring break," Jasmine said.

"About then," the doctor said.

She continued to talk, but Nina was still trying to come to grips with what she'd already said. How could she be pregnant? It was one night, and she was on the shot and—

Her heart stopped for an instant. She hadn't gotten the shot the last time. She'd been too busy studying and had meant to get it at a later time. But somehow, it had slipped her mind. It just wasn't a priority when she wasn't in a relationship, and now, she was pregnant. Would Alex be furious at her for not taking precautions? Had he asked her if she was on the pill?

She couldn't remember. The night was a blur of sex, decadent treats, and pampering beyond her wildest dreams.

"Are you alright?" Jasmine asked.

Nina smiled at the doctor, faking a calm she didn't come close to feeling.

"Thank you, Doctor. Can I go home now?"

"Of course. Just make sure to schedule an appointment as soon as possible and choose a regular doctor. You're going to need care often."

"Thank you," Nina said, but the busy ER doctor was already gone.

"You're pregnant with a billionaire's baby," Jasmine said. "Holy shit."

"That's exactly what I was thinking."

"What are you going to do?"

"I'm going find a doctor. And I'm going to have to call Alex and let him know."

"What do you think he's going to say?"

"I don't know."

"You didn't make this baby by yourself."

"I know, Jazzy. Just calm down."

"I'm trying to be calm, but I'm freaking out a little."

"Me too," she admitted.

She stared at the picture of the tiny little heart, wondering how the little bean could possibly be the start of life, but the truth remained the same. She was pregnant, and Alex was the only possible father. Her life was about to change in a big way, and not the way she'd been hoping. She was pregnant with Alex Conrad's baby. She had to tell him, and give him a chance to weigh in on whatever decision she made. She'd taken a chance with a wild night, and it had blown up in her face. But she had to face this head-on, and that started with telling Alex.

Chapter 5

Nina turned the card over in her hand, her phone sitting on the desk in her dorm room. She looked at the clock, shocked it had been less than twelve hours since they left the room for commencement. It felt like a lifetime since that morning, and Nina felt infinitely older. There was nothing she could do now to change what happened, and she had to deal with it today. By Friday, they had to be out of campus housing, and she needed to find an apartment quickly, so she didn't spend too much of her savings on hotels.

"Just get it over with," Jasmine said from her bed, looking almost as worried as Nina was.

"Do you think I can have a moment? I don't know what to say, but I feel weird having this conversation with an audience."

"It's fine; I get it. I'll take a walk and come back in a little bit."

"Thank you, Jazzy."

"I'm a text away if you need me."

"I know."

Jasmine hugged her, then left quickly. Nina waited for the door to close, then dialed the number and held her breath while she waited for him to answer.

"This is Alex," he said, his voice all business.

Nina cleared her throat, reaching for what she wanted to say, but she was struggling.

"Hello?" Alex said, as if the connection was bad.

He was about to hang up when she finally found her voice.

"Alex? It's Nina."

"Nina?" he said. "From spring break?"

She was shocked he remembered her, but also a little flattered.

"Are you coming back to Florida?"

"Not exactly."

"Oh. Then, why are you calling? I haven't heard from you since you left, so I figured that you weren't interested. Is something wrong?"

"I'm sorry about that. I got wrapped up in my senior year and I just lost track of time."

"Did you graduate?"

"Summa cum laude."

"Congratulations. That's something to be proud of. What did you major in, again?"

"Accounting."

"I guess I'm confused. If you're not calling because you're coming for a visit, then why are you calling?"

She took a deep breath, but after a long moment of silence while she came up with a better way to say what she needed to say, she decided to just spit it out.

"I'm pregnant."

"Congratulations."

"Alex, you're the father."

There was silence on the other end. Nina was panicking. Would he demand that she end her pregnancy, or would he insist that it wasn't his? Would he be angry with her for forgetting her birth control? Or would he think she did it on purpose to trap him? When he finally spoke, his calm voice was shocking.

"Do you have a plan, yet? I'm assuming you just discovered this yourself."

"I found out today. And no. I don't have a plan. I was planning on going to interviews all week and getting a job. I just got out of college, and this was not in my plans."

"Understandable. A driven woman like you usually doesn't plan on a baby like this. I'm sure you're freaked out. Who wouldn't be?"

She didn't know what to make of what he was saying, but she was so relieved that he wasn't angry, or denying that he was the father that she was beyond words. She'd been ready to defend her own honor, but he took her word on it and seemed comfortable doing so. He was wildly different than any man she'd ever known.

"Can I offer a suggestion?" he asked, voice still eerily calm.

"Of course. This is as much your baby as mine."

"I'm glad to hear you say that. Look, I'm in need of an accountant on my payroll I can trust, and there's plenty of room in my home if you want your own space. I can pay you whatever the market is for your profession, plus free rent, food and your own car."

"Alex, I couldn't—"

"The car would be in your name and one hundred percent yours. The way my house is laid out, you can live in your suite and never see me if that's what you want. And I can give you the suite with an in-suite office, and your own patio access to the yard. The only thing you wouldn't have is your own kitchen. If not, I have room for a guest house."

"That's really generous, but I can't."

"Why not? You said this baby is just as much mine. Doesn't the child deserve a father? I'm not saying we have to get married or that we even have to sleep together. That's just not how I work. You can stay here until you get on your feet and move out and get another job if you want. I'm offering you a solution; how permanent it is depends on you."

"I don't want to be in a position where I'm dependent on you."

"And you won't be. Look, Nina. You're a sweet woman, and truth be told, I was hoping you'd call. Not for this reason, but just because. I haven't ever been with a woman like you, and I think we can make this work. Maybe this baby is a sign."

"A sign? Don't you think that's a little over romanticized?"

Alex laughed.

"I don't think anyone's ever accused me of being overly romantic before."

"I wouldn't say *overly* romantic," she said, thinking about the first-class tickets and the box of fancy chocolates.

"I seem to remember you enjoyed my type of romance."

She could feel the heat rising as he spoke. How did he get to her so easily? His voice was like silk, and he drove her wild with just a few words. Could she live in the same house as him without jumping in bed with him every chance she got?

She laughed. It didn't matter. She was already pregnant. Sleeping with him now wouldn't be an issue. It was getting her heart broken that was the danger.

"Laughter is good, right? What do you say, Nina? Work for me, help me keep my finances straight and move in with me?"

"And what will I do after the baby is born?"

"You'll work when you want to, just like now. I'm offering you a salaried position."

"But if I move on and find more work, I don't think 'managing my baby daddy's finances' is a valid reference."

"Conrad Companies International is an excellent job refence, and with over ten billion in assets, I would think that being on my staff would give you a leg up should you seek employment elsewhere."

"If I didn't want to live with you, would I still be able to take the job?"

"Of course, but why would you want to work in an office when you could work from home, take a boat out on Biscayne Bay whenever you want, and swim to your heart's content on your breaks? I love spoiling you."

"I remember."

"Give it a month. If you hate it here, I'll pay to fly you back. How much do you want salary-wise?"

"One hundred thousand a year," she said without hesitation, even though her current prospects were closer to the sixty thousand range.

"I can pay that," he said. "That's roughly eight thousand a month. That's more than enough to get you started if it doesn't work out and you want to move back to Kentucky. Plus, if you leave, I'll be paying support for the child. That's another ten thousand a month I'm sure."

"You don't have to do that."

"I do. I'm going to take care of you and our child whether you're here or in Kentucky."

She took a deep breath, not sure what she should do. It was a huge leap of faith moving in with him. But like he said, she could leave any time. And, living with him came with a job. So, it wouldn't be like she was dependent on him. Because she could walk away whenever she wanted to. Or she could get her own apartment. It was all up to her.

"Okay," she said, almost in a whisper.

"Okay you'll come here or okay I can pay you child support to live in Kentucky?"

"I'll move to Florida. But only for a month to start. If it doesn't work out, I'm on the first plane out of there."

"Deal. How soon can you have your things packed?"

"They're already packed. I only had a few days left on campus anyway, so everything is packed."

"Is tomorrow morning soon enough to fly out?"

"I have a little more than two suitcases worth of stuff."

"That's fine."

"I have like ten boxes."

"No problem. I'll send a car for you in the morning."

"I can drive to the airport myself."

"I know you can, but I don't want you carrying boxes around when you don't have to."

She started to argue, then changed her mind. She was exhausted and struggling with nausea in the mornings. There was no reason to push herself to the breaking point again.

"You know what, you're right. Thank you, Alex. I'll see you tomorrow."

"I look forward to it," he said, then the line went silent in her ear.

Jasmine must have been right outside the door. As soon as she hung up the phone, her friend was there, waiting for the details.

"I'm moving to Florida," she said.

"Are you sure?"

"I can come back if I don't like it. He has a house there, and he needs an accountant anyway. I think it will be the best thing for both of us."

"And what about me?"

"You can visit anytime you want, Jazzy. You know that."

"Don't you think this is a little soon?"

"I do, but I'm pregnant. Better now than waiting until I give birth. He deserves to be there for that, and I'll make sure that you're there, too. Jazzy, I know this is hard, but please, just be happy for me."

Jasmine blew out a long sigh.

"Alright," she said, nodding. "I'm happy for you. He just better not break your heart or I'll have to kick his ass."

"I'll make sure he knows."

"And I want to see you often."

"I'll make sure that happens."

"Oh Nina. I hope you know what you're doing."

"I don't, but this feels right. As scared as I am, it just feels like the right choice."

"Please be careful."

Nina hugged her friend, squeezing her tight and kissing her cheek.

"I will," she promised. "I will."

Chapter 6

It was early the next morning when there was a knock at her door. She looked through the peephole, not at all surprised to see a man in a smart uniform smiling on the other side.

"I'm here for Miss Nina Wilson," he said, then stepped back so she could open the door.

She did, already dressed in her powder blue suit that Alex had bought her, a bright yellow shirt giving it just the right pop of color for a more casual look. She finished the cracker she'd been nibbling on to curb her nausea, then grabbed a can of ginger ale and dropped it in her purse.

The man wasn't alone. Another man in a similar uniform was pulling a dolly, obviously there to pick up her things. She motioned them into the room, pointing out the boxes that were hers and then hugged Jasmine one more time before hurrying out of the room. They'd spent most of the night dealing with their emotions, and this morning, Nina had woken up ready to face the day. Jasmine, not so much.

She followed the men downstairs, surprised to see a small moving truck and a limo. When the driver held the door for her, she got in and sat in the comfortable back seat. Watching the university buildings fade away, then seeing the airport loom, she wondered if she would find herself back in Lexington again anytime soon. Part of her hoped so, but that would mean that their relationship had failed. Nina was willing to give their love a solid chance at blossoming from its humble beginnings, if only for the sake of her unborn child.

The airport was busy, so it was no surprise to Nina that the limo driver skirted the heavily traveled lanes and made his way down a more private road. Nina had made peace with the privilege that the rich enjoyed, and she fully expected getting to the airport and through security would be easy. Carrying the lovechild of a wealthy man had its perks. What she wasn't prepared for was the limo driving right onto the tarmac and pulling up right beside a private jet with the moving van right behind them.

The limo driver opened the door and offered his hand. She took it, holding only her purse and staring at the Bombardier Global 6000 welcoming them, staircase already lowered.

"What's this?" she asked, though she already suspected.

"Your chariot," the man said, smiling.

"Wow. I thought I'd be flying first class, but this is off the chain. I wish Jasmine could see this."

"Would you like to see the inside?"

"I would."

The man smiled then walked behind her up the stairs, his hand on her back in a kind gesture meant to steady her. She took the stairs slowly, but the vertigo she'd felt before was gone thanks to the medication she'd been given. Still tired, she felt so much better than she had before.

She stepped onto the plane and gasped, taking the lush seating in the first section, then the dining room and sitting room in the next two sections.

"Have you been on a Global 6000 before?" a voice behind her asked.

She turned, the pilot standing where the limo driver had been before quietly slipping away.

"I haven't," she said.

"Let me give you the tour. Here are the chairs for takeoff. This model has four chairs in this section, and two more chairs suitable for takeoff and landing in the dining area. Behind us is the galley. They can whip up just about anything that you can think of, so don't hesitate to ask for things that aren't on the menu. The flight is about five hours, so if you get hungry, just let the flight attendant know."

"Should I pick my seat now or are they assigned?"

The pilot chuckled.

"You're our only passenger. Well, you and your boxes, which will go in the luggage compartment. You can sit wherever you want. Once we hit cruising altitude, you can take advantage of the sitting area with a large couch that pulls out to make a bed and a flat screen TV. Just beyond that is the bathroom, which features a shower and a makeup vanity with a chair."

"Seriously?"

"Yes."

"Wow."

"It looks like your luggage is loaded. Would you like to take a seat and peruse the menu?"

"That sounds lovely."

"Alright. We'll be taking off soon. If you need anything at all, don't hesitate to ring the flight attendant. We are here to make your flight comfortable, so no request is too large."

"Thank you."

He left, leaving her to sit in the soft, leather chair next to the window. She settled in, watching the plane speed down the runway. She was reeling. Alex had chartered an entire plane just for her? It seemed insane. When the moving truck had appeared, she thought that her stuff would be driven down while she flew. It seemed like the logical choice, and since Miami was a fifteen-hour drive from Lexington, it made sense. Now that her things were on the plane and she was the only passenger, she felt like she was dreaming. Was this how the other half lived?

It's so quiet, she mused, leaning back and sighing. *A girl could get used to this.*

The takeoff was smooth, the plane soaring into the sky and into the clouds with ease, then leveling off. The seatbelt sign turned off and almost immediately, a petite brunette in a flight attendant's uniform appeared from the galley.

"My name is Jessica, and I'll be your attendant for this flight. Can I get you some refreshments?" the woman said, her smile genuinely sweet and not the thin, stressed smile of someone who made their living wrangling two hundred passengers per flight.

"I would really just like a turkey sandwich and some ginger ale."

"There is a selection of breads listed on the back, do you have a preference?"

Nina flipped the menu over.

"You have all this on the plane?"

"Yes ma'am," the woman said.

"You know what, surprise me."

"Excellent. I'll be a few minutes. Would you like to take your meal in the dining room or the sitting room?"

"Sitting room," she said, just now considering that option.

She'd intended to eat right at her seat.

You're not in coach anymore, she thought, almost laughing out loud as she watched the attendant walk away. *You're not even in first class anymore. This is insane.*

She made her way through the dining room and to the sitting room, turning on the TV and scrolling through Netflix until she found a movie that looked interesting. Before she'd had a chance to get comfortable, Jessica reappeared with her meal, setting it on the coffee table with her drink.

"Wow, Jessica, that looks divine."

"If you don't like avocado I'll make you another, but I promise you, this is the best turkey sandwich you'll ever sink your teeth into."

"It's perfect. Thank you."

Jessica smiled and nodded her head slightly, then she disappeared, her heeled shoes silent on the lush carpet. Nina took a bite out of the sandwich and moaned softly. Jessica was right. She took her time, savoring every bite, then finished off the fancy chips that were obviously made from exotic, colorful potatoes. Then she kicked back and put her feet up on the coffee table so she could enjoy the movie.

She was starting to doze off when she heard Jessica gathering her dishes.

"It was wonderful," Nina said.

"I'm so pleased you enjoyed it. Are you tired? Would you like to lay down?"

Nina tucked her feet up onto the couch and smiled. Her shoes fell to the floor and just as quickly, Jessica had scooped them up and placed them in a cubby under the TV.

"This is good enough."

"There's no such thing as good enough." Jessica laughed. "I'm not here to make your experience passable."

"A bed would be nice."

"Excellent. You can stay right there."

Confused, Nina sat up, feet still tucked beneath her. Jessica pressed a button just above the couch, and the coffee table lowered about a foot before the foot board on the couch rose up and then extended. In under a minute, the sofa had transformed into a queen-sized bed, all without the part she was sitting on moving. The back of the sofa and the arms remained.

"It's almost like my grandmother's pull-out couch," Nina mused.

"Except this is more like your favorite spa chair and your grandmother's couch rolled into one." She handed Nina a remote. "There's a button for a light massage while you sleep, heat, and cool. You can also elevate the back of the sofa so you can see the TV better."

"This is amazing."

"I'm glad you like it."

She opened a cabinet and pulled out a large down comforter and a pillow. Nina moved to help her, but Jessica shook her head.

"You're too sweet," Nina said.

"There's no such thing," Jessica said, tucking the blanket around Nina after placing the pillow behind her head. "I'm going to close the door and leave you to rest. There is a button to turn down the lights and the red button will summon me if you need anything."

"Thank you, Jessica."

"My pleasure."

Nina snuggled down into the covers after turning on the low heat and the massager. For the first time in a long time, she felt completely at ease. Alex was going to take care of things. He was going to take care of her. Maybe their relationship would never grow beyond friendship, but she had no doubt that he was going to make everything right. Whether it was with her living in his house in Miami, or living on her own, Alex wasn't going to walk away from his responsibility. This mistake wasn't going to ruin her life, and she was going to gain work experience in the process. If she walked away, at least she would have that.

She'd told Alex she was committed to at least a month, but she was going to give it more time than that. At least three or four months while they hashed things out and learned more about each other. He was practically a stranger, and that was going to take some time. For herself and for this baby, she was willing to give herself and Alex more grace than she normally would in a new relationship. After all, she was going to have to deal with him in some way for the rest of their child's life. Wouldn't a happy ending to what was a whirlwind of a romance be the best outcome? It was definitely the outcome that Nina was hoping for, and it was the one she and her baby deserved. Alex appeared to feel the same way.

The heat and massage had her asleep in minutes, and before she knew it, a gentle hand was shaking her awake.

"Sorry, Jessica," she said dreamily as she opened her eyes. "I must've fallen asleep."

"I'm not Jessica," a male voice said, chuckling.

Nina blinked, Alex's face appearing in front of her.

"You slept through the landing," he said. "Jessica didn't have the heart to wake you up."

"How long have I been asleep?"

"A little while." He smiled, brushing her hair away from her face. "I enjoyed waking you."

"Are you going to get charged for the holdup? I'm sorry. And you didn't have to charter an entire plane just for me."

Alex laughed, the sound sending tingles up and down her spine. He was exactly how she remembered him. So full of life and genuinely happy. She was glad to see her pregnancy hadn't changed that, even if he was laughing at what she'd said.

"Why is that funny?" she asked, slipping on her shoes while the bed retracted.

"I just can't wait to show you what life can be like. Your innocence is refreshing, and I know I'm going to enjoy spoiling you."

"My innocence about what?"

"Everything." He kissed her tenderly, then held out a hand to help her onto her feet. "Don't worry about them charging me for the delay."

"I just didn't want to cause you any issues."

"There is no issue," he said, putting his arm around her as they made their way to the car that waited on the tarmac of the small airstrip. "It's my plane."

Chapter 7

"This car is amazing. I've never been in a car that has a leg rest before."

"It's a Mercedes Maybach Security Edition."

"What does that mean?"

"It's bulletproof, among other things. And the partition between us and the driver isn't just for privacy. If someone does manage to carjack the driver, this compartment is only operational from inside here."

"That's insane. Like a panic room inside your car?"

"Basically."

"Why do you even need that?"

He shrugged.

"I move a lot of money around. This is faster and more secure than hiring an armored car every time I have precious cargo." His smile was mischievous as he continued. "But the biggest selling point for me was the mini fridge right here between our seats."

Nina was shaking her head.

"Some of this luxury is out of control."

"Why?"

"It seems a little over the top."

"You won't think that when you're moving money to my accounts and you know you're safe in here."

"I'm going to be moving your money?"

"Typically, no. I have guys that do that. But there may come a time that I need you to step in, or even audit the money I have. Most of your work will be done from home, but your car will be similarly equipped so that I know you're safe."

"I don't know about someone driving me everywhere."

"That's my preference, but it is up to you. If you're going to be driving yourself, I'll have to rethink the car I was planning to give you."

"You don't have to give me a car; I can buy my own eventually."

"You can't buy one of these. Outfitting a luxury car with state-of-the-art security isn't something just anyone can buy. Besides, it's part of your salary package and I want you and my child to be safe."

His hand went to her belly, his touch so gentle that it made her heart swell. Why had she been nervous to tell him about the baby? It was simple, she realized. His reaction was wonderful, but he was virtually a stranger. She had no way of knowing how he would respond, and even now, everything was up in the air. Things were good, but she needed to guard her heart in case they went south once the newness wore off for both of them.

"That's fine. It's more important to me that I'm able to drive myself places than it is to have everything go my way."

"I'm glad you're willing to compromise. It's a good quality in a woman."

She glared at him, then she realized that he was joking.

"Funny," she said, but she was laughing.

She didn't expect him to be so real, and every time his personality showed she felt more at ease with their situation.

"Are we still in Miami?" she asked as they made their way from what was obviously a private airstrip through the city.

"We are. We're in a suburb of Miami called Coconut Grove."

"It's beautiful."

"Wait until you see where I live. Where *we* live."

He took her hand in his, kissing her knuckles and looking into her eyes.

"Are you nervous?" he asked.

"A little. But mostly, I'm hoping this works out."

"Me too. I appreciate you giving us a chance instead of running off on your own or using the child as a pawn."

"I'm not that kind of woman. My mother taught me to own my mistakes and never make other people pay because I'm angry. I've carried that lesson over into everything I do."

"Your mom is a brilliant woman."

"Was. Both my parents are gone."

"I'm sorry for your loss."

"Thank you. It's been a few years, but it still hurts."

"I lost my mom when I was young, too. I was seventeen."

"What about your father?" she asked, squeezing his hand warmly.

"I never knew my father. It was just me and my mother."

"I'm sure she would be proud of you."

"Thank you. I hope so. Everything she did was to get us out of Little Havana."

"Little Havana?"

"I know that sounds crazy since I'm white, but my stepfather was Cuban, and my mom moved in with him in a little peach house on Twenty-Third Street, not even ten miles away from here. It's a world of difference, isn't it?"

"That's crazy. Was he good to you?"

"While he was alive, yes. He did his best, taught me how to get things done, and how to be a man. He was good to my mom and he took care of us. When he died, he left everything to her. It wasn't much, but he owned his house outright, and that made a huge difference when it was just me and my mom."

"It's amazing you were able to pull yourself out of that so young."

"I'm twenty-eight, so hardly a child."

He chuckled.

"That's not what I mean. It's just a rough way to start adulthood, all alone like that. I had Jazzy when I lost my parents."

"Being alone made it easier. I was able to focus on my goals and not worry about how they affect other people. I would give anything to have her back, but she and my stepdad gave me all the tools I needed to pull myself out of our humble beginnings."

"Do you still have the house?"

"I do. I renovated it and made it into a community center."

"That's amazing of you."

"I wanted to give back to the place that made me the man I am today."

"That's noble of you." The car turned, and she looked out the window as they made their way down South Bayshore Lane. "Is that the ocean?"

"No. It's Biscayne Bay."

"These houses are amazing."

"I'm glad you like them."

The car turned again, and Nina looked at him, eyes wide.

"*This* is your house? This isn't a house, this is a mansion."

"You could call it that."

"And the bay is right there?"

"I have a dock at the end of my property."

"This is insane. I can't believe I'm going to live here."

"You're going to like it here, I promise."

She was almost breathless as the large, wrought iron gate opened to reveal an intricately laid cobblestone driveway. The landscaping was lush, with local plants lining both sides of the driveway so that the ten-foot stone wall that surrounded the entire property and the neighbors beyond were not visible through the trees. The gate closed behind them, and the Maybach drove down the circular drive to park next to a large fountain.

"Alex, this is amazing."

"You've said that a time or two. Wait until you see the inside of the house."

"What is that building there?"

"The detached garage. And above it is a four-bedroom apartment complete with a kitchen. The garage holds six cars. Your car can be parked in the garage, or if you prefer, there is a carport near the back exit."

"The back exit? How big is this place?"

"The property or the house?"

"Both."

"The property is nearly five acres. The house has twelve bedrooms and eleven bathrooms, five common areas, two kitchens and three dining areas."

She stared at him in shock. Alex smiled.

"Would you like to take a quick tour of the grounds?"

"Please."

Alex sent a quick text and the car rolled forward almost immediately.

"The swimming pool is lighted, and temperature controlled. You can swim year-round, and the jacuzzi is also temperature controlled so you don't have to worry about it getting too hot. The garage has three doors on either side of the building so that all cars are accessible without moving the car behind or in front of it. There's a balcony that runs around the entire second floor."

"Am I living in there?"

He laughed.

"No. That's where my drivers live."

"They live here?"

"I have two drivers that live here full time. I also have a few security guards that live here also. Two live in the garage apartment with the drivers, and two live in the back of the property near the boat dock, and the other two live in the main house. I have one cook and one cleaning lady. Both are available to help you at any time."

"Why do you need so many guards?"

"It was safer than hiring a firm to deal with the money. A lot of these professional wealth-management firms have been screwing their clients. It's easier for me if I run my business from my offices and my home. That way, I don't have to worry about someone sneaking in under my nose and taking what I've worked so hard for."

"I guess you don't get to be a billionaire by being trusting."

"Not one bit. We have two boats on our personal dock, as you can see."

"It's like a fortress here."

"It is. Which is important. Having high-dollar houses all lined up like this puts us at risk. You can sleep safe knowing that you are completely enclosed."

"It's nice that you can't see the neighbors or hear the street."

"Isn't it? It's like living on a private island. There are two suites available. You can take the suite on the bottom floor with courtyard access, or you can take the suite on the second floor. It has a wonderful view of the bay, and the balcony runs along the entire suite so you don't have to go through a specific room to get to it."

"Can I look at them first before I choose?"

"Of course. The only thing that makes the first-floor suite better in my opinion is the extra room off the nursery for a nanny, and it's near the kitchen."

"I don't need a nanny."

"Are you sure? I was waiting to hire someone until you got a chance to interview them, but having help is never a bad thing."

"Are you planning on being involved?"

"With the baby? Heavily. But we'll both be working, and I don't want you to exhaust yourself."

"I don't know how I feel about a nanny."

"Then don't get one. I won't be offended."

"Thank you."

He gathered both of her hands in his.

"Listen. I want you to be happy. I want more than that, but right now, your happiness is my greatest concern. If you don't like anything, or if you want something I haven't provided, speak up. Promise?"

"I promise."

"Good." He pointed out a narrow walkway lined in the same cobblestone pattern as the driveway. "There's the walkway. It's lighted as well, and meanders through the property so that one trip around is a mile. This branch of the driveway here leads to the Vista Court, which will take you to the main road. It's a dead end so there's only one way to go."

She was taking it all in, storing the information away for later as they made their way back to the fountain and parked. She had no idea when she was going to need all the information he'd given her. One thing was abundantly clear; Alex Conrad was very security conscious, almost to the point of paranoia. It was either going to make her feel very safe or trapped, so she was going to have to make sure that she felt like she was in control of her life.

She would start by swallowing her pride and accepting a security enhanced car rather than having to rely on drivers to get her everywhere. The more control she had there, the less likely she would feel like she was stuck here. It was a small thing, but she knew it would make a difference. The other thing was that she was going to set up a bank account the next day at a bank that Alex had no vested interest in. She doubted he was wanting to mingle finances, which she wouldn't want to do anyway, but she also wanted to make sure that she could walk away without any strings.

You're giving up before you even get started, Jasmine's voice said in her head, and Nina knew it was true. But she didn't have it in her to be careless with money. She wanted a backup plan just in case, and there was nothing wrong with that.

Alex led her up the small flight of stairs where a man was waiting at the door. He wore a crisp black suit and looked more like a secret agent than a doorman. Something about him was familiar.

"Jaime?" she said, smiling.

He didn't smile back.

"Yes."

The smile slipped off her face, but he was already opening the door and she wasn't sure he saw her frown.

What a dick, she thought, walking through the door and gasping when she saw the lavish entryway to the house.

"Wow."

"I'm glad you like it," Alex said. "You said you wanted the second story suite, yes?"

"I think so."

"Good. It's near my room." He motioned to the ornate spiral staircase in front of them. "Shall we?"

The staircase led to a landing, which had a small kitchen and dining area. The dining area looked out onto the lower floor and a large window behind the staircase that stretched from the floor of the first story to the top of the second story held a view of a beautiful courtyard with a fountain filled with koi and brightly colored parrots in the trees.

"This is the family kitchen and dining room. The main kitchen and formal dining room are on the ground floor on the other side of the courtyard."

"Does anyone use this kitchen?"

"I use it for breakfast. I like to eat here or on the balcony before I get dressed in the morning. It makes no sense to go all the way to the formal dining room, then come back up here to change."

It was her turn to laugh.

"Must be nice."

"If you would like, you can leave a list of what you would like in this kitchen, and I'll have it stocked with what you need. Or you can eat what the chef makes."

"Being rich seems to make things really complicated," she teased.

"I find that speaking your mind cuts down on a lot of that."

"You keep saying that, but I don't think you want to know what I'm thinking all the time."

"Try me."

"Alright, but I'm not going to apologize when you don't like what I have to say."

"I wouldn't have it any other way."

She laughed.

"Good. We can start now. I really want to see this suite."

"Right this way," he said.

He held out his elbow and she took it, sparks flying between them. They went across the landing to the hallway that was to the right of the dining room and kitchen.

"To the left is the rest of the second level. There are five bedrooms on the first floor; three of them are suites. The first-floor suite is the one I offered you, and it's meant to be the Master Suite, but

I like the view from up here better. I'm sure you'll see plenty of my suite, so let's skip it and I'll show you your rooms first."

A chill passed through her when he mentioned his bedroom, his meaning obvious. She had to admit that she was happy that he'd mentioned it. She didn't want to make the first move and he was far too polite to assume that she owed him anything just because they'd slept together before.

The hallway was short, ending with a set of double doors similar to the large, dark wood doors that had led into the house, and into the suite. He opened them with a flourish, and stepped back so she could take it all in.

"Is this my room?" she asked, shocked by the size of the empty space.

"No. This is the sitting room. The first door on your left is your office, the second door is a half bath. Through the door straight ahead is your bedroom, and on the back wall is the bathroom, walk-in closet, and nursery respectively."

She walked through that door as he spoke, in awe of the space that could fit a small house.

"This is too much," she whispered.

"Not at all. Nothing is too good for the mother of my child."

"Alex, I don't know if I can accept this."

"You'll get used to it," he said, pulling her close and hugging her.

She felt so safe in his arms, his strength enveloping her and warming her to her very soul. How could she accept so much from a man she barely knew?

"Let me spoil you," he said quietly. "I want you to be happy here."

"This is a big move."

"I know."

"I don't know if I'm ready for this."

It felt strange to admit it, but it was the truth. More than once since their conversation the day before, she'd wondered what in the world she was thinking. *How could she pick up everything and just move? What if he expected more out of her than she was willing to give?*

"If I stay it doesn't mean that I'm automatically your girlfriend."

"I expected nothing less."

"I deserve to be courted and pursued."

"I agree."

"And I don't want business and pleasure mixing."

"I wouldn't dream of it."

"I want to have set hours so that I'm not at your beck and call at all hours."

"Understood."

"Why are you smiling?"

"You're so sexy when you're firm."

"You're out of control." She laughed.

"Only when you're around."

"You're not the only one," she admitted, then smiled when his nostrils flared at her words and his eyes widened ever so slightly. He was aroused and probably had been since he picked her up from the airstrip.

She shook her head, looking around the empty room.

"What about the furniture?"

"I thought you might like to decorate yourself," he said.

"Are we going to a furniture store?"

"Nope." He pointed to the built-in bookshelf beside her.

"Is this a catalogue? It's bigger than a phone book."

"You can order individual pieces or complete sets. Or, you can choose your colors and what types of furniture you want, upload a picture of the room on your cell phone, and they'll design a custom room for you. It's entirely up to you."

She flipped through the book as he talked, one perfectly manicured eyebrow lifting when she saw the high-end pieces on the glossy pages and something else caught her eye.

"There are no list prices."

"Price doesn't matter." He looked at his watch. "It's three o'clock now. If you order in the next two hours, the stuff will be delivered and set up by dinner, which is at seven."

"What am I supposed to do while I'm waiting for everything to arrive?"

"I have an idea," he said, pulling her into his arms again and kissing her roughly.

She melted into him, holding her body against his and delighting in his heat. When he let her go, she smiled seductively.

"I think I know exactly what you have in mind."

Chapter 8

When Alex opened the intricately carved doors and stepped aside to let her in, she gasped at the sight before her. His suite was laid out similar to hers, starting with a well-decorated living room with doors on either side. The carpet was so thick she felt like she was walking on air, the rich, dark blue the same color as the bay, which was visible through the bank of large windows that took up the entire east wall. Automated curtains lowered with the touch of a button on the wall, and soft, sensual lighting from recessed light fixtures filled the room.

The furniture was high-end, the fabric soft beneath her fingertips as she ran her hands over the back of the large section as she walked by it. A large tabletop fountain trickled quietly from the corner, adding to the feeling of calm the blue hues and subtle pops of color already gave the room. The decorating style was very masculine, with clean lines and neat edges, but somehow still very welcoming. Nina could lose herself in a room like this.

"How do you ever leave this room? It's so beautiful."

"It's nothing compared to the bedroom."

He held out his hand and she threaded her fingers through his. Lightning shot through her body at his touch, just like it had that first night. The connection they shared was so intense, it was like nothing Nina had ever experienced. Alex was nothing like any man she'd ever met. He was strong, yet kind, funny, driven, yet relaxed, and he was obviously good with money. His mere presence set her at ease and lit her soul on fire. It was a combination that Nina found incredibly sexy.

"What?" he said, and she realized that she was staring.

She ducked her head, turning away a little.

"I'm embarrassed that you caught me," she admitted. "But you are just—"

"Sexy, funny, amazing, perfect?" he teased.

She laughed. She couldn't help it.

"Well, I obviously got funny right."

He pulled her into his arms, kissing her soundly, then pulling back and looking at her with a warm smile on his face.

"I love the way your face lights up when you laugh, Nina. I hope you'll always be this happy here."

He brushed a strand of hair off her cheek and tucked it behind her ear. She shivered beneath his touch, closing her eyes and enjoying the feel of his hand on her skin.

"I hope so, too," she said.

His hand went to her stomach, resting gently on her still soft curves and leaning in to kiss her again. She opened her mouth to him, her body already humming with need. She pulled away and smiled at him.

"If you keep doing that, we're not going to make it to the bedroom."

"I have a feeling that's going to happen a lot. I can't seem to control myself around you."

"Same," she said, then giggled when he scooped her up and carried her through the bedroom door.

He laid her gently on the bed, then lay beside her, green eyes smoldering as he pushed the blazer of her pantsuit open, then off. Propped up on one elbow, he looked down at her while he slowly traced his finger over the swell of her breasts beneath her shirt, then down until he reached the hem. He pulled it up and over her head, revealing a matching yellow bra beneath.

"Pretty," he whispered.

He ran his finger over the lacy edges, then dipped into her cleavage and unhooked the front clasp with ease. The fabric fell away and he leaned down, taking one hardened nipple into his mouth and sucking gently. Nina's head rolled back and she moaned. She wrapped her arms around his head, pulling him closer and arching into him. Alex took the hint, pulling harder with his hot mouth until her moans turned to desperate little squeals.

Just when she thought she couldn't take anymore, he switched to the other side. This time, he didn't ease into it, and the sensation was wilder than before. Her hands grabbed the sheets, twisting them as she struggled to control her traitorous body.

She writhed beneath him, but he didn't relent. When he started kissing down her belly, she realized that at some point, he had slipped her pants off while she'd been focused on what his mouth was doing to her breasts.

She knew where he was going, but still wasn't prepared for the sweet flow of heat that rushed to her loins when he pushed her legs open and ran his tongue between her already swollen folds. Her fingers slipped into his hair and she held on, opening her legs and arching her back. He circled his tongue around the tiny, sensitive nub of flesh, his hands holding her hips so she couldn't move away from the overwhelming pleasure.

"Alex," she said, too lost in the pleasure to say much more.

He chuckled and the vibration set her nerves aflame. Her hips were moving of their own free will now, desperately pressing against him and silently begging for more. She wanted him inside her, but when she pulled at him, he didn't budge. He was in no hurry, and he wasn't going to be persuaded no matter how much her body pleaded.

When she tensed and froze, Alex doubled down, plunging his tongue inside her an instant before she started trembling, then exploded with the most powerful orgasm she'd ever experienced.

She cried out his name, her movements frantic as the pleasure ripped through her. Her back arched and her breath was coming in quick gasps.

When she finally fell back onto the bed, he released her, leaving a trail of kisses on her stomach and working his way up to kiss her neck and shoulders. She wrapped her arms around his neck and kissed him boldly, then hugged him tight against her.

"That was amazing," she said.

"I thought a little welcome to my home was in order."

"You're still dressed."

"I like it this way. Maybe I'll impose a nude workday and visit your office several times a day to make sure you're complying."

She laughed, but the thought had her body twitching again. *How was she ever going to get any work done with him right down the hall?*

She got her answer in the next moment when his phone rang from the nightstand beside the bed. He groaned and rolled over.

"Sorry," he said.

"It's business hours," she said, shrugging. "It's no big deal."

"You're amazing," he said, kissing her quickly, then grabbing the phone.

"Bueno."

Nina was shocked. She hadn't realized he spoke Spanish, but even though she didn't understand a word, it was clear as the short conversation progressed that he not only spoke Spanish, but spoke it fluently.

He said goodbye and hung up, his face already conveying the coming apology.

"Duty calls," he said. "But if you want to relax until your suite is finished, you can stay here and watch whatever you want."

He took a remote out of the nightstand and pushed a button. A massive flat screen slowly emerged from the floor a few feet from the foot of the bed.

"That's a really big TV."

"Don't rush out of bed. I don't expect you to work this week. Just concentrate on getting a feel for the area and how the house runs, okay?"

"That sounds good, but hold on."

He stopped in the doorway and turned.

"What?"

"I just—You speak Spanish? I thought you were white."

"I am white." He laughed.

"You speak Spanish like a native."

"I grew up in Little Havana, remember. Everyone there speaks Spanish."

"Oh."

"If it turns you on, I'll speak Spanish to you all day long."

She laughed.

"No. I was just really surprised, and then I wondered why you would know Spanish. I like a good mystery."

"Mystery solved, then. Look, I have to take care of something. I don't know when I'll be back, so don't wait for me if you get hungry or want to take a walk around the grounds or something. The house staff will sign for your shipment and ensure that it is assembled and placed properly. Make yourself at home."

"Alright. Thank you."

He was still standing in the doorway, staring at her. When he rushed toward the bed suddenly, she tensed. But he was only coming back for one last kiss before he had to leave. He was gone in the next instant, and Nina was left in the middle of his huge bed, naked, and totally satisfied.

She lay there for a long time, finally deciding to take him up on his offer to make herself at home. Grabbing an oversized, chenille robe hanging on the back of the bedroom door, she made her way through the living room to the large bathroom, which was completely separate from the toilet.

"I gotta remember this," she said out loud, daydreaming about a home like this of her own in the future.

Not the entire mansion, but a nice sized house with a welcoming family room and a large bedroom. *And* a bathroom that was just for bathing.

The room was larger than her college dorm room had been, and like the other rooms, the east wall featured a huge bank of windows that overlooked the Biscayne Bay. A large jet tub was directly beneath the windows, the breathtaking view visible from the reclined seating built into the tub. Nina started filling the tub with warm water, putting some bubble bath into the water flowing out of the tap.

The air filled with the scent of honeysuckle that smelled so true to life that Nina almost expected to turn around and find a tree right in the bathroom. But it was only the fragrant bubbles that were filling the tub. The ledge was lined with glass bottles that held various bubble baths, body washes and shampoos, each labeled with a simple description on the front in the same silver letters on frosted glass. Even the tiniest detail was pure luxury, and Nina was tempted to request a set for her own bathroom. But she wanted to provide for herself as much as possible while she lived here, so until then, she would stick with what she could afford.

The entire bathroom was more like a spa than a room in someone's house. Every inch was created for the ultimate bathing and relaxing experience, right down to the seating area beneath a heat lamp in a reading nook. She was going to have to take advantage of that area, too.

The tub filled and water turned off, she slipped into the warm bath and sighed when the seat cradled her body just right.

This is the life, she thought, watching one of the neighbors untie their boat from their personal dock at the back of the property. Alex's house had a private dock as well, which held a *Pershing 5x*. Smaller than some yachts, it was built for speed and maneuverability.

The only reason she recognized the model was because Jasmine had almost convinced her to get on one during spring break, but Nina wasn't willing to pay fifty bucks to be crammed onto a boat that was already overfilled and had seen far too many drunken parties in its lifetime. Alex's boat was pristine, looking almost like a postcard on the well-maintained dock in the sparkling bay.

She exited the bathroom a long time later, freshly scrubbed, dry hair clipped up and out of the way, dressed in her pantsuit again. She made a mental note to make sure she unpacked her clothing first so she would have something to wear. It wasn't like she could walk down the hall in a borrowed robe and go in search of her bags. Alex probably hadn't meant for her to roam the house naked when he said to make herself at home.

She laughed at the image, carefully hanging up the robe again and closing the double doors behind her as she left Alex's suite.

Her stomach growled and she made a beeline for the stairs, heading down to the main kitchen on the first floor. It was nearly time for dinner, and she was hoping that Alex's promise of gourmet dinners served nightly started tonight. She was starving, and she realized that she hadn't had a thing since her turkey sandwich earlier in the day.

Working her way down the winding stairs carefully, she went straight at the bottom of the stairs and quickly got turned around. Nothing looked familiar, and the door at the end of the hall, which she'd expected to be the formal dining room, turned out to be an office of some sort. She backed out as soon as she realized her mistake, closing the door as she did and turning to get her bearings.

She almost ran into Jaime when she took her first step. He was standing in the hallway, watching her with arms crossed.

"Can I help you?"

"I was looking for the kitchen."

He raised an eyebrow, clearly mocking her.

"What were you doing in the study?"

"I told you, I was looking for the kitchen. I'm hungry."

"The kitchen is that way."

"I'm sorry. I got turned around."

"Didn't you get a tour of the house just an hour ago?"

"What is your problem?" she asked, resisting the urge to point a finger into his large, overly pumped up chest. "It was an honest mistake. I'm hungry, not looking for a damn office."

He didn't move, didn't apologize. She glared at him, his dark brown eyes challenging her to mess with him. She'd forgotten exactly how rude he'd been at the club, and now that she was moved into the house, he was acting like she was invading his territory. But he was huge, he had a gun, and Nina was starting to feel lightheaded now.

"Look, I'm sure you don't care, but if I don't get some food in the next few minutes, I'm going to get sick all over this nice carpet. So, if you could move out of the way so I can find my way to the kitchen, I would appreciate it."

"Alex wouldn't be happy to know you were snooping in his office while he was away on business."

"I'm sure I can explain myself. Now, please, move."

He stepped aside and pointed in the direction of the kitchen again. She ignored the jab, and the way he was acting like she was hiding something and walked right by him without another word. Maybe he was threatened by her being there. *Was it possible that she was stepping on his toes, or filling a job he'd had his eye on?* Or maybe he had assumed that she was trying to use the pregnancy to trap Alex. She couldn't blame him for being suspicious. Plenty of women intentionally got pregnant to trap wealthy men. It was one of the oldest tricks in the book.

But Nina had a lot more self-respect than that, and she'd just been so busy with school that she'd forgotten her shot. If Jaime wanted to believe the worst of her, that was on him. She only cared what Alex thought of her. She was carrying his child, not his bodyguard's. Jaime was being ridiculous.

She turned, about to confront him so they could clear the air and not do this every time he saw her without Alex present. But even though she hadn't heard him move, he was nowhere to be seen. She was alone in the hallway.

For some reason, that was more unsettling than turning to find him staring at her would have been. Curious and a little on edge, she hurried back to the office door, quietly trying the knob and finding it locked. Was Jaime in the office now, or had he locked it and disappeared through another door during the few moments she'd had her back turned to him?

She tensed, expecting to find him when she turned again, even though it was impossible for him to have gotten in front of her. The hall was still empty, and now, she was freaked out. Hurrying as fast as she could without running, she made her way down the hall and turned left at the staircase, which was where she'd gotten turned around in the first place. There was no telling what Jaime was up to, but he was huge, a little scary, and he was downright mean. She didn't want to run into him alone again. Ever.

When she found the kitchen and formal dining room, she let out a heavy sigh. The table was already set, and the household staff along with the guards were already finding a place at the banquet table, ready to eat before the shifts changed.

One of the men she'd seen in the yard earlier noticed her right away and motioned her over. He stood and pulled out an empty chair beside his seat, then waited for her to sit before pushing the chair back in.

"Thank you."

"You're welcome. Dinner will be out soon. Can I get you something to drink?"

"I would love some ginger ale."

"Coming right up," he said.

He was smiling when he hopped out of the chair and went into the small kitchenette where a refrigerator, cabinets filled with dishes and a single sink were. She could see from where she sat that the refrigerator in the kitchenette was solely used for soft drinks and bottles of water. He opened the door to every drink imaginable, selected a can of ginger ale and handed it to her when he returned to the table with it and a fancy wine glass he'd grabbed from the cupboard.

She would've happily drank straight from the can, but she didn't have the heart to tell him that ginger ale poured into a wine glass was a little extra. He was kinder than Jaime and he was trying to be nice. She had a feeling that Alex had prepared them for her arrival and laid the law down, but only Jaime seemed to be bothered by it. Everyone else at the table was smiling at her, and it appeared that everyone knew exactly who she was.

The attention was a little overwhelming, but before it got to her, the food came out and her mouth began to water.

"What is that loveliness?"

"Pot roast on mashed red potatoes with truffles and mixed summer vegetables."

"Truffles?"

"Not the chocolate; the mushroom things they find with pigs."

"I know what a truffle is. I just didn't expect to be having it with dinner. Does everyone eat like this every day?"

"Of course. Alex treats us like family, and food is fuel. There's a selection of healthy, gourmet meals twenty-four hours a day. And if you have a request, they'll work it into the rotation."

"What about turkey sandwiches?"

The man stopped, fork poised a few inches from his mouth. He stared at her.

"Turkey sandwich?"

"I'll have to grab the recipe the flight attendant wrote down. It wasn't just any old turkey sandwich."

"I'll have to try it," he said, but she had a feeling he was humoring her.

She smiled and changed the subject.

"Do you live here, too?"

"I stay in the carriage house during my down time. It's a sweet gig, and it beats the hell out of commuting from the affordable side of Miami."

"Where's that?"

He laughed, shaking his head.

"It doesn't exist. Besides, where else are you going to work with a warm bed, three gourmet meals a day and every streaming service you can possibly imagine on the televisions?"

"It does sound pretty sweet."

"Alex treats his guys good. That's why we're all so loyal. This is our family, and family sticks together. You'll get used to it."

She took a bite of the roast, closing her eyes and savoring the rich, hearty taste that was better than any roast she'd ever tasted.

"See what I mean?" he said, chuckling. "I put my life on the line every day to make sure that Alex and his interests are safe. You can't buy that kind of loyalty with a turkey sandwich."

Chapter 9

Nina was already up and ready to go when her first day of work rolled around almost a week later. She opened the door, surprised to see Alex waiting for her in the hall.

"You can come in," she said. "You don't have to knock."

"I know, but I want to respect your space, too. I know that this was a big decision for you, and I think a little respect goes a long way."

He caught her arm and pulled her in for a quick kiss.

"I thought you were respecting my space." She laughed.

"I'm a good guy, Nina, but I'm not a damn saint."

"I'm almost ready."

"You don't need to bring anything. I'm just showing you the properties today."

"I want to get things organized in my laptop. This will help me get an idea of where to start."

"Suit yourself. Can I help you with anything?"

"You can carry my laptop if you want," she said. "I'm sorry, that was rude. I would appreciate it if you carried my laptop downstairs for me."

"My pleasure."

His crooked smile had her body in knots, but she ignored it. If she gave into the feeling now, they'd never get any work done. She'd spent the better part of the last week in his arms, and it was time for her to buckle down and start earning her keep. She wasn't here to mooch off the rich guy; she was here to see if they could make it work for the sake of their child, and pad her resumé in the process.

So far, everything was going better than she expected, and Alex was the kind, caring man she'd thought him to be. That didn't mean she could just give up control and trust it would always be this easy. She was an independent woman, and the best part was that Alex understood and embraced that part of her.

They got into the back of the Maybach and she caught Alex looking at her.

"What?"

"You're just so different when you're all business. You're in control and in your element. I like it."

She sighed.

"It is refreshing to be around a man who isn't threatened by my confidence."

His laughed filled the small space as Jaime pulled the car through the open gate and turned right on Bayshore Lane.

"Are you kidding? It's one of the things that first drew me to you. You were out there on that floor, dancing alone without a care in the world, completely oblivious to everyone around you."

"I didn't realize Jasmine was gone." She laughed.

"But even when I asked you to dance, you were all class. Look, Miami is a party town and some of the people who come here have no self-respect. They're just looking for a quick lay until they head back home. And the locals, well, a lot of the women that frequent my clubs know that my VIP section is a veritable who's who of the wealthy and eligible. They're on the hunt from the moment they walk through those doors, and it's painfully obvious."

"Thirsty."

"Exactly. But not you." He put his hand on her thigh, squeezing affectionately. "You give off this vibe that called to me from across the packed room. I could see you right away, even though you were surrounded by more people than that dancefloor is meant to hold. I knew if I wanted to convince you to go upstairs that I would have to do more than wink at you. You're not like other women, Nina. You're amazing and I'm so glad you walked into my club. I can't imagine my life if that moment hadn't happened."

His words touched her, and her heart swelled.

"You made quite an impression on me, too."

"I noticed." He was holding her hand now, bringing her knuckles to his lips and kissing them softly. "I pulled out all the stops, and you didn't call me for months. It's the first time that's ever happened."

"I should have been eating out of your hand, what with those chocolates, the first-class upgrade, and everything else."

"But you weren't. You did eventually call, but it was completely unexpected."

"I feel bad about that. I should have at least called you and thanked you for everything."

"It worked out. You're here now."

"Because I'm pregnant."

"Like I said, it worked out."

He kissed her hand again, and butterflies started dancing in her stomach.

"How are you for real?"

He shrugged.

"You're not the only one that refuses to be someone you're not, no matter what society thinks. Life is too short to leave things unsaid."

The car pulled off the highway, stopping at a small, but well-maintained hotel within walking distance of the beaches but away from the crowded streets where vacationers tended to gravitate.

"This place is nice," she said, pulling out her phone and taking a picture before using her maps app to pin the location.

"What are you doing?" he asked, handing her a ginger ale from the mini fridge while they waited for Jaime to park the car.

She opened it and drained the can, then handed it back to him.

"I want to make sure I have a picture and address for each location's file folder on the laptop and hardcopy."

"No hardcopies," he said. "But I like that idea. It will make it easier to keep everything organized."

"That was the plan. Did you say there are no hardcopies or that you don't want me to keep hardcopies?"

"Both."

She wrinkled her brow.

"Why?"

"We're a green company."

"Oh. I didn't realize that."

He shrugged.

"I know that people don't think of hotels and the tourist industry in general that way, but we do what we can. That includes avoiding paper use."

"I'm glad you told me. I would have had hardcopy files on every property by the end of the week."

"Glad we avoided that little mishap," he said, getting out of the car and going around to her side.

She opened the door and took his hand when he offered it, leaving the laptop in the car and taking just her cell phone. The air outside the car was already a balmy seventy-five degrees, even though it was still early in the morning.

"You look sexy in that outfit," Alex said just as Jaime walked around the front of the car.

Nina caught Jaime rolling his eyes, but she ignored him. He obviously didn't like her, and that wasn't her problem.

"I liked that pantsuit so much, I decided I needed one in every color."

"Well, lavender is definitely your color."

"You'd say that if I was wearing a paper sack," she teased, earning another eye roll from Jaime.

"True. Come on, let's get started. I think you'll find our operations run surprisingly well, even though I have most of my cash offices running independently."

"How many properties?"

"Twenty-two," he said.

"That's a lot."

"They're not all hotels, and some of the hotels are pretty small. The hardest properties to deal with are going to be the three luxury hotels. They bring in a lot of cash every day. That's why I need you to come through and streamline the process."

"It's going to take some time."

"I understand," he said. He held the door for her while Jaime scanned the surrounding area. "I'm not looking for miracles, just a better system than the one we have."

"That, I can do."

"I'm sure you can."

Without a word, the man behind the desk jumped up, greeting Alex and hitting the buzzer to let him behind the desk. Alex typed his password into the keypad, making sure that Nina was watching so she could add it to her file. She made a note on her phone, then followed him into the room, which shut automatically behind them. Jaime remained in the lobby, visible from the monitors in the cash room that cycled through the cameras throughout the entire three-story hotel.

Alex watched Nina input names into her phone, taking a picture of the two employees that were in the cash office.

"I thought you were putting all this on your laptop?"

"I am, between properties. My phone has an app that syncs with the laptop program, so I'll upload all this information as I create each property's file. It will make it go so much faster, and I can spend my time working on the important things, rather than organizing information."

"Smart. I'm impressed."

"Thank you. It makes it easier to work with things." She addressed the clerks in the office. "Can you show me how your accounting system is set up?"

One of the clerks looked at Alex and he nodded. Nina watched him, chalking his discomfort up to feeling put out. She didn't blame him; he was probably used to doing things a certain way, and she was a newbie, coming in and shaking things up without warning.

They spent almost an hour at the first property, and by the time Nina was back in the car with her laptop sitting on the little tray that folded down from the partition that separated the rear seats of the heavily armored Maybach from the front seat, her mind was already churning.

"We're going to visit the rest of the properties, but we won't spend nearly that much time. I want to make sure everyone knows who you are, and that you have the entry codes and addresses for every property. It will be up to you to visit each property this week and get the files you need."

"I can do that," she said, already getting excited. "I have so many ideas right now."

"Well, don't push yourself too hard. Like I said, I don't expect a miracle, but I would like to look at my properties and know exactly how much I've profited over all, rather than having to review each property on its own."

She left the laptop open, sitting back in the chair and watching the palm trees sway out the window.

"This place is magical," she said.

"Do you feel at home, yet?"

"You know what? I do. Thank you. Everything seems to be falling into place so perfectly."

"I'm glad to hear it."

It was several hours later when they pulled into the last property. This time, a gas station. Nina left the laptop on the tray, getting out without waiting for Alex to help her.

They ran through much of the same information they had at the small hotel, the general manager of the gas station friendly and just a little loud. Nina instantly liked him. She took the information she needed, including the location and code for the cash office, then headed outside ahead of Alex to get some air before they got back into the car. They'd been in the car most of the day, and even with a lunch break, Nina was starting to feel the effects of sitting in a moving vehicle all day.

A single SUV pulled into the parking lot, but the station was otherwise deserted.

That's odd, she thought. There was another gas station across the highway, which seemed to be doing plenty of business. She thought it was odd, but chalked it up to direction. Traffic was heavier on the southbound side at the moment, which meant it was probably pretty packed on the northbound side in the mornings, which was where they were.

It made sense since easier access from the highway would affect business. She made a note in her phone to always visit this station after the morning rush so she didn't get stuck during a busy time, then she headed for the car.

A man got out of the SUV, pressing the buttons on the pump, then grabbing the nozzle. Nina realized she must be exhausted, because she hadn't even seen him put a credit card into the slot. She watched him for a second, wondering why he looked so familiar, but she couldn't place him before he turned around to pump his gas.

Alex opened her door for her and she got in, syncing the information from the station before finally leaning back and putting her feet up.

"Sorry about the long day," he said when he got into his seat.

"It's only been eight hours."

"Yeah, but I'd prefer it if you kept your days around the five-hour mark."

She pursed her lips, then shrugged.

"I guess I shouldn't look a gift horse in the mouth," she said. Jaime pulled out of the parking lot and she caught a glimpse of the gas station sign. "Wow, gas is high in Miami."

"Fill up is free here," he said.

"Does that guy in the SUV work for you?"

"He does."

"That's why he looked familiar."

Jaime eased the Maybach onto the highway, heading southbound in the heavy traffic. Nina was looking absently out the window when she spotted the other gas station's sign and wrinkled her nose. It was almost fifty cents lower than Alex's station. She almost said something, then thought better of it. She had no idea why the prices were different, and the brand of gas Alex sold wasn't one she'd heard of. It was possible it was a high-end fuel, which would explain the difference. Besides, she wasn't there to tell Alex how to make the money, she was just there to count it.

"You'll see a lot of my guys at that station. I prefer to fill my cars with my gas."

"That makes sense. You wouldn't want to have your money going to the competition."

"Exactly. Anyway, like I said, I don't want you working more than four or five hours a day, and this week, you can just focus on getting everything together. Once you have a system worked out, we'll figure out how to link the properties with your laptop so you don't have to do too much driving around to get the job done."

"I can do that."

"I know you can. Now, that's enough talk about work."

"What do you want to talk about?"

"You. How are you feeling?"

"I'm good."

"That's it, just good?"

"Trust me, 'good' is great when you're pregnant. I feel better than I have in a few weeks. I'm entering the second trimester, so I think that's why I'm starting to feel like myself again."

"That's more like it," he said, leaning across the seats and kissing her on the cheek.

He opened his mouth to say something else, but before he could, his phone rang. He sighed.

"My apologies," he said, then answered the phone in Spanish.

Nina listened, wishing she'd paid attention in her high school Spanish class, but the only things she could pick out were yes, no, and good. Not exactly helpful. Excited to have something to challenge her outside work, she decided to download an app on her phone. *Might as well learn Spanish while I'm working part-time*, she thought, turning the phone so Alex didn't see what she was doing.

She wanted to surprise him. If they were going to raise this baby together, it only made sense that they would teach the child Spanish. It wasn't Alex's native tongue, but she could tell growing up with a Cuban stepfather had shaped who he was as an adult. Their baby was due around Christmas, and if she worked really hard, she might be able to surprise him by then.

She smiled, setting the permissions and starting an account. The app even came with a voice recording feature, which meant she would be able to record herself attempting to copy the prompts. It was worth the ten dollars she'd just paid in the app store. Now all she had to do was contain her excitement until she was alone so she could get started.

Alex was going to be so surprised, she just knew it.

Chapter10

Nina sat back in her office chair, letting out a huge sigh. It had taken her all week, but she'd finally managed to get all the accounts organized and current, giving her a place to start now that she was keeping Alex's books. She looked at the number at the bottom of the overview page, which showed a staggeringly high number. All-combined, Alex's properties had brought in nearly a billion dollars just in the last quarter.

She had been expecting a number closer to half that, but after running the numbers three times, she came up with the same number. Even the gas station that they'd visited was doing surprisingly well. Despite what unorganized money handling and properties that varied wildly in size and overhead, every business appeared to be doing extremely well. Even the restaurants, which were notoriously risky business ventures, were pulling massive profits.

It was like Alex had the golden touch.

Her phone chimed at her and she rolled her eyes. The app she had downloaded had been prompting her to spend a couple minutes learning new words each day. She'd been putting it off, so busy with work that she just hadn't had the time. She had no time after work either, since Alex knocked on her door most days at five, making it a point to have dinner with her and the rest of the crew in the formal dining room. By the time she had a moment to herself, she was usually ready for bed.

She started to click the snooze on the notification when she stopped herself. *I've got to learn Spanish*, she thought, forcing herself to open the app for the first time since she'd downloaded it. It was clear from phone conversations that Alex had pretty much daily that many of the people he worked with spoke Spanish.

She wasn't sure if they spoke English as well, but a common language went a long way towards establishing rapport. It would only help her, and once she got proficient enough, she could practice with Alex.

Excited again, she opened the app, perusing the menu and clicking *Lesson One*. She went through the lesson several times, repeating after the prompt and doing her best to imitate the audio example. By the time she felt confident that she had the first lesson mastered, it was almost four o'clock.

She laughed when the screen filled with colorful fireworks, congratulating her for completing the first lesson. It was silly, but it made her feel like she accomplished something. She made it a point to do at least one lesson a day until she completed them all. It would take her months, but it was worth it.

A dialog box appeared on the screen.

Would you like to translate your recordings? the prompt asked.

"It recorded me?" She laughed, shaking her head.

She wasn't sure she wanted to hear it. Would she sound ridiculous? She clicked *yes* too curious to let it go. Maybe she would be pleasantly surprised, or maybe she would have all the motivation she needed to keep at it.

When the menu popped up, she realized that she had several recordings, each with a date and time stamp from the past week.

"That's odd," she said, clicking on the oldest recording and immediately recognizing Alex's voice.

At first, she was spooked, then she realized that she had given the app permission to record. Like other apps, even when it wasn't in use, it was always on in the background. While social media apps used keywords in overheard conversations to target ads to the owner of the phone, this app apparently started recording the instant it recognized someone speaking Spanish.

"So, that's what I paid all that money for," she said, listening to Alex's smooth voice as he spoke to the person on the other line.

The recording ended, and another dialog box appeared.

Would you like to translate?

She hesitated, then clicked *yes*. If it was private, he wouldn't talk about it in front of her, right? He had no way of knowing if she understood the first time he'd done it, so it was probably just business.

Another screen popped up and the recording started playing while English subtitles scrolled across the empty black screen.

"This is so cool," she said, reading along while listening to his voice and the way he was pronouncing the words.

She recognized a few words from the first lesson, but the rest of the conversation was a blur and made no sense without the other person's side of the conversation. It was a cool feature, but she needed to use it when there were more people involved.

She was about to hit the x to close the screen when one line caught her eye. Using her finger to rewind the video, she read the previous sentence, then the sentence that had piqued her interest again.

Just give her the cooked books when she comes. No, she doesn't know, but I need a viable financial file for each property just in case.

She paused the recording and rewound it again and again, reading it with a sinking heart. He had to be talking about her, right? There was no one else that he could be talking about. She moved the slide on the video back a few more sentences, but none of that made any sense at all, and it was clear that they'd been talking about something else when the person on the other line had blurted out their question about Nina.

She pushed *play* again, letting the video finish out, but there was nothing else that caught her eye.

She looked over her shoulder, suddenly paranoid as she pulled out her earbuds and closed the office door behind her. She pressed the thumb lock down and sat back in her chair. With one earbud in so she could hear if someone knocked, she scrolled through the files until she found a more recent one. This file was dated two days, and the time stamp showed it was pretty late at night.

She thought back and realized that she had spent the night in Alex's bed after a wild night of sex, and she was sound asleep during this call. Not sure what she was going to find, she clicked the button to translate and another blank screen popped up and the words began to scroll across the screen.

She sat there, open-mouthed, trying to make sense of what she was seeing. This conversation was clearly about her, but nothing else really made sense. It started with, "No, she's sleeping," which meant he absolutely had been talking about her.

She nearly jumped out of her skin when the door handle turned part way, then stopped. She pushed the button on the side of the phone to lock the screen and hurried to open the door.

"Was the door locked?" she asked when she opened the door to Alex's smiling face.

"I was about to ask you the same question. Did you press the button down by mistake?"

She made a show of looking at the knob, then smiling as if embarrassed.

"I didn't even notice it was there. I probably did. Force of habit after living in the dorms for so long."

"I bet," he said, hugging and kissing her as he always had when he came up after his workday. "What's wrong? You seem distracted."

"I am," she said. "I've been working all day and guess I'm still thinking in numbers."

"We talked about that. I hope you're planning on scaling back your hours when you're done setting up the system."

"I will."

"How much longer do you think it will take?"

"At least another week," she lied.

"I'm in no hurry. I'm surprised you've gotten to the halfway point. This baby is going to be a genius if he's even half as smart as his mom."

"He?" she teased, jumping on the opportunity to steer the conversation away from work. "How do you know that it's not a girl?"

"Wishful thinking," he said, kissing her again.

This time, she leaned into the kiss, even though she wasn't feeling it. Alex was lying about something, and she needed to get to the bottom of it before this went any further. But Alex needed to think that nothing had changed so he would keep doing what he was doing. She needed answers, and she knew that Alex was smart enough to be more cautious if she acted like she suspected he was up to something.

"Dinner is a little early tonight," he said. "I have a surprise for you."

"What is it?" she said, putting her phone and earbuds in her pocket.

"If I tell you, then it's not a surprise. Don't worry, you're going to love it."

He put his elbow out and she took it, letting him lead her down the hall and to the dining room. When they were almost to the dining room she stopped, smiling apologetically.

"I need to use the bathroom," she lied.

"I'll save you a seat," he said.

He kissed her on the cheek and left her standing in the hall outside the bathroom. She hurried into the room, locking the door and unlocking the screen on her phone. She scrolled through the menu on her app, starting the recording and making sure that it worked when the screen was locked. It did. She put her earbuds in the other pocket and got her phone situated with the microphone facing up, then flushed the toilet and turned the faucet on and ran her hands under the water.

She washed with the fragrant soap that was selected specifically to enhance the décor of this room. Everything in the bathroom was a deep red, so naturally, the soap smelled of warm apple pie. The house staff took as much care with every room in the house, and Nina had to wonder at the amount of wealth it would take to make her care whether a room that was mostly warm browns and off-whites should smell like vanilla or cinnamon.

She opened the door to the bathroom and stopped herself in time to avoid a collision with Jaime. She scowled at him, but he didn't acknowledge that he had nearly run her over. He just kept walking. She bet he was in on it, too. Whatever *it* was.

She had a lot of thinking to do when she found a moment to herself after dinner and whatever surprise Alex had in store. First, she needed to know what he was hiding from her, and then she had to decide what, if anything, she was going to do about it. Would it be worth it to get involved if it was something small?

What if the thing he was hiding was his net-worth? Did he want to make sure she was in it for love and not money? Was he drafting a prenup? Or maybe he was doing something else entirely, and once he exposed the truth, she would find out that the truth was nowhere near as bad as she'd thought it would be.

She followed Jaime into the dining room, heading straight for the empty seat next to Alex. Their meal was already being served and the table was filled with familiar faces. Nina watched the people around her as some ate quickly and left, relieving the guards still on duty that were waiting for their turn. The staff worked like a well-oiled machine, and it seemed like everyone knew exactly what they were supposed to do without fail.

Now that she was feeling suspicious, she noticed that they behaved with military-like efficiency, and she found herself wondering why Alex needed all these guards. Sure, it was obvious that he was wealthy, and moving money from his properties could be dangerous, but he had a full staff of men that appeared to serve no other purpose than to watch the house. Sure, some of them had job titles that suggested they were just your basic house staff of the super-rich, but even the gardener and the car mechanic looked like they could take down an elephant with their bare hands.

"When are you leaving?" she heard Jaime ask Alex from the seat on the other side of him.

She remained focused on the people around her, but her ears were trained on their conversation.

"We'll leave in an hour."

"I should go with you."

"I've got this."

"You put yourself at risk traveling alone."

"I'm not worried about it. It's only a couple of hours."

"You won't even know I'm there."

Alex laughed, and she could see Jaime's hand tense.

"Of course, I will. It's fine, Jaime. We have everything we need and the weather is perfect."

"Suit yourself," Jaime said, his frustration palpable as he calmly got up from the table and started to leave.

"Where are you going?"

"To make sure everything is ship shape so I don't spend the night worrying about you."

"Jaime, you are too good to me. Everything will be fine."

"For my peace of mind—"

"Fine. Check everything and make sure we're good to go. It can't hurt to have a second set of eyes."

Jaime nodded curtly and walked away, his foul mood leaving the room with him.

"What was that about, Alex?"

"He worries about us."

"Not us, you. He doesn't like me."

"That's just how he is. You have to look past his gruff exterior to see the heart of gold he's trying to protect."

"If you say so."

"I've known him for five years. He's a good guy. I trust him with my life and yours, too."

"Does he know where we're going?"

"No, which is why he's wound up about it. I want it to be a surprise. It's been too long since I've spoiled you."

"I've been here less than a month and you've bought me a car, new wardrobe, and furnished a private apartment in your home for me. I think you've spoiled me plenty."

Her stomach clenched, and her own words made her feel guilty. She was trying to catch him in a lie when he'd given her no reason not to trust him. It wasn't about them personally, just his business. Could she really expect him to know her for such a short time and just tell her everything?

She felt bad now, the phone in her pocket heavy with her guilt. Maybe she'd misinterpreted what was going on, or maybe the translating app wasn't that good. There was something lost when translating from any language to another; that was common knowledge.

She couldn't be sure that the translation was one hundred percent accurate until she had more information, and even if it was, everything she'd read had been out of context. What if Alex overheard a conversation between herself and Jazzy; would he be suspicious or come to conclusions that were wrong?

She didn't know the answer, but she knew it was possible. She still felt like something was going on, but she didn't know what. Until she had more proof, she wasn't going to let it ruin a perfectly good surprise.

Chapter 11

When Nina returned to her room while Alex went to change, she discovered a pile of neatly folded clothes on her dove gray sofa and a pair of shoes. Startled that someone had been in her living room, she thought back and couldn't remember if she'd looked at the couch on her way out of the room to dinner. Had Alex put them there before going to the office?

She decided that was likely the case, and she'd been so distracted by her suspicions that she had completely missed it. Now that she thought about it, she even remembered that he had been on her right when they left, completely blocking the view of her sofa with his body.

Relieved that she had explained her suspicions away and kicking herself for thinking every little thing was something more, she took the tags off the clothes and held them up to look at them. They held no clues to her surprise, but it was clear that they were going somewhere that required comfortable clothes and flat shoes.

Intrigued and a little excited, she hurriedly got dressed, admiring her reflection in the mirror. Alex had really good taste in clothes, and everything he'd ever picked for her had made her feel like a goddess. This outfit was no different. The khaki slacks and pale pink shirt were understated elegance, the shoes comfortable the instant she slid her feet into them.

A soft knock on the door announced Alex's arrival. She opened the door and he sucked in a quick breath.

"Is there anything that doesn't look good on you?"

She smiled, leaning into his quick kiss.

"I can't wait to see what has you so excited."

"You're going to love it," he said.

He took her hand and led her out of the room, down the stairs and out the side door that led to the courtyard.

They meandered down the walkway, through the beautifully landscaped yard toward the back of the property. The wind was light, the breeze just enough to soften the late afternoon heat. Nina could smell the salty sea air, and hear the birds flying over the water. When they stopped at the back gate and Alex opened it to lead her to the dock, her excitement grew.

"Is this the surprise?" she asked, breathlessly.

"Yes. You like?"

"I love."

She could hardly contain her excitement as she walked alongside him to the yacht. He helped her onboard, then untied them from the dock and pushed off, leaping onto the deck and taking her into the main cabin.

He took the captain's seat, turning the engine on and slowly pulling away from the dock. He patted his knee and she sat on his lap, taking the wheel and steering the yacht in the direction he pointed.

He wrapped his arm around her waist, holding her steady as they flew across the water heading east. Sunlight streamed through the panoramic skylights and warmed her bare shoulders.

"Where are we going?"

"Just around Biscayne Bay." He pointed to a spot out in the water, away from the private docks. "We're going to drop anchor there, then I'll show you your surprise."

"*This* isn't the surprise?"

"I really love you," he said.

She felt him tense beneath her, and she reached down to take his hand.

"I'm sorry. Was it too soon?"

"If that's how you feel, there's no such thing as too soon."

"I think I've known for a long time." He took a deep breath. "Not to be trite and overly sappy, but I knew when I saw you. The way you laughed and the way you carried yourself, I just knew that you were the one for me."

"Hold up, you're not bringing me out here to propose, are you?"

He laughed, wrapping his arms tighter around her and snuggling against her.

"*That* would be too much right now. But when you're ready—"

"That's a long time down the road."

"I'm not worried. We've got the rest of our lives ahead of us. You're worth waiting for."

He slowed the boat, taking control with Nina still seated on his lap. When he found the perfect spot, he engaged the anchor and helped her up, leading her to the sundeck. He opened one of the storage areas, pulling out a picnic basket and a large, green bottle.

"I can't drink, I'm pregnant," she said when he opened the bottle and began pouring the golden, bubbling liquid into a champagne flute.

"It's sparkling apple cider," he said, handing her a glass then pouring his own.

"Thank you."

They leaned against the pillows on the padded sundeck, and Alex started removing treats from the basket.

"Wow," she said. "You really went all out."

"I thought it would be nice to have dessert, enjoy the view, and just have a moment where we're not surrounded by dozens of people."

"It is a little weird having so many people underfoot twenty-four hours a day."

"Does having your own suite help?"

"It does. It's like an apartment, and I can walk onto the balcony and just enjoy the bay and the fresh air without having to go through the entire house to get outside."

"But?"

"What gave it away?"

"There's something you're not telling me. Is someone bothering you?"

"Not bothering me, it's just, well, it's Jaime. He acts like I'm ruining everything, but I'm not sure what I'm doing wrong."

"Nothing. Listen, Jaime and I go way back. He was a bouncer in the first club I ever bought, and he has been through some crazy stuff with me. He's like the brother I never had, and he's really protective."

"I didn't ask to come here."

"I know that," he said, smoothing her hair out of her face. "And he knows that. But it's in his nature to be suspicious of everything. That's what makes him so good at his job."

She took a deep breath, inhaling the salty sea air and listening to the gentle waves lapping against the hull while she tried to put into words what she was trying to say. It was more than he thought, but she couldn't put her finger on the issue.

"I think he thinks I got pregnant on purpose," she said before she could change her mind.

"So, what? Who cares if he thinks that?"

"I care. That's not what happened at all. I had my life planned out and this totally threw me off my game. If he thinks I wanted this, he's wrong." She looked at him, shaking her head and covering her mouth. "I didn't mean that how it sounded. Damn, I'm sorry, Alex. I love it here, I really do. You're the best thing that ever happened to me."

"But you didn't plan for this."

"I didn't. And I'm not really good with going with the flow, as I'm sure you've noticed. That's why I'm an accountant. Numbers never change and numbers don't lie. I'm much better with numbers than I am with people."

"You seem pretty good with people to me," he said with a wry grin.

"You know what I mean. You get me, but people like Jaime; they make me feel like I'm constantly doing something wrong just by breathing."

"I'll talk to him."

"No!" She took a breath. "I'm sorry, I mean, please don't. I don't think that will help at all."

"You're right, it probably won't."

"It's going to take some time, I just wish that he didn't act like I was some gold digger trying to snatch you up."

"That wouldn't bother me."

"Alex, I'm being serious."

"So am I. If my money is what you noticed first and that drew you to me, then so be it. The thing that matters to me is that you're here now, you're happy, and our baby is happy and healthy."

"You're a hot mess."

"And you love it."

"I do," she said, sipping on her sparkling cider and looking out onto the bay. "What's that little island there?"

"I see you like to change the subject when things get too deep."

"I'm not even going to deny it. But really, what is that place? It's beautiful."

"It's the Key Biscayne. There's a national park there, and this area is filled with wildlife. I thought you would enjoy seeing the more natural side of Miami. We're more than just parties and beaches."

As if to punctuate his remark, there was a splash not far from the boat.

"Whoa, was that a dolphin?" she asked.

"It was. That's not all there is, but once the animals settle now that the engines are off, they'll start coming out."

He produced a ribbon-wrapped white cardboard box from the basket and opened it. He took one dark chocolate dipped strawberry out of the box and held it to her lips. She took a bite, closing her eyes and savoring the rich, dark flavor.

"That is divine," she said, taking another bite and licking a small piece of chocolate from her lips.

Alex's sparkling green eyes were locked on her mouth, watching each bite.

"I'm glad you like them," he said in a voice gone husky.

"They're perfect. This is perfect, Alex. I feel like the luckiest woman in the world."

"Not as lucky as I am," he said.

His meaning was clear, and he was being sincere. He meant it when he said he loved her earlier. His words made her heart race, and she knew that she felt the same way. She just wasn't sure if she could say it yet.

Another dolphin shot out of the water, doing a little flip and playfully splashing nearer to the boat. There was more movement off the port side, and when Nina leaned over the edge a little to have a closer look she gasped softly.

"It's a sea turtle," she said in a near whisper.

"I should bring you snorkeling out here another day," he said. "There are a lot of animals to see here."

"This is amazing."

"I should have brought you out here sooner. It really is a magical place."

"I can almost see your house from here. I can't believe this is all so close."

"*Our* house."

"Thank you for saying that. I really do feel at home with you."

She took a strawberry out of the box, feeding it to him as he'd done for her, kissing him deeply when he was through.

"You taste so sweet," he said.

She smiled.

"Is there a below deck I should see?"

"There's so much more to see."

"Are we still talking about the boat or something else?"

She arched one delicate brow in question, handing him her empty glass and taking the hand he offered to help her. His touch was electric, the heat that rushed through her felt like the first time.

She followed him to the lower deck, body already trembling with need. The large living quarters were luxurious, just like everything else in Alex's life. But Nina was focused on Alex, hungry eyes roaming over his tight body, the light streaming through the windows making him look more like a god than a mere mortal.

"You look like you're about to ravage me."

He laughed, but when her hands went to his belt buckle without a word, the smile slid off his face and was replaced with a look of pure desire. She had him undressed in a few moments, shoving him down onto the bed and throwing her shirt over her head. Stepping out of her pants and her shoes in one motion, she crawled onto the bed and straddled him, kissing him hungrily and sliding herself onto his erection.

"Wow," he breathed, leaning back and watching her as she rocked her hips against his.

"I'm sorry," she breathed. "I just, I just needed you."

"I like it."

He reached up and cupped her breasts, squeezing, then rubbing his thumbs across her nipples. Her head rolled back and she moved even faster, completely focused on her own desire.

"That's so good, keep doing that."

"You're beautiful when you're horny." He chuckled.

Her body was on fire, her breathing so shallow that she was gasping, but her orgasm was looming, and she wasn't letting up until she came.

When she noticed Alex go quiet she looked down, smiling.

"Looks like I'm not the only one," she all but purred.

She leaned forward, bearing down and taking him to the hilt, her eyes locked with his, the power of being the one in control feeding her lust. She laced her fingers through his and held his hands on either side of his head, pinning him down so he was completely at her mercy.

"I love you," she said, admitting what had been on her heart for so long.

She kissed him before he could say anything, then wrapped herself around him, and buried her face in his neck just before the climax overtook her. Trembling around him, she whimpered his name and he pulled her closer. He cradled her against his body and arched his back. Thrusting deep, he finally let out his own cry of triumph, spilling his heat into her body and kissing her hungrily, over and over again.

When she collapsed in his arms he held her there, the gentle swaying of the boat rocking them softly.

"That was amazing," Alex said, brushing her hair away from her forehead and giving her a tender kiss. "Anytime the urge comes over you, I'm your man."

She laughed along with him, then she went silent for a moment before turning serious.

"I meant what I said."

"I know."

"I've known for a while now, but I didn't want to admit it."

"Why?"

"I'm not that woman this kind of stuff happens to."

"What kind of stuff?"

"Being swept off her feet by a charming prince with millions in the bank."

"Technically, I'm a billionaire, so there's that."

She laughed.

"You know what I mean. I'm always so careful and I plan everything out. I didn't see this coming."

"You can't plan for love. That's not how it works for anyone. Trust me, when I saw you on the dance floor, I was not in the club to find a woman. I was there enjoying the success of my most recent investment. But I did see you out there, and you took my breath away. I knew the minute I saw you that I needed to know your name. That seeing you was more than just a chance encounter. It was fate, and I truly believe that. You're perfect for me, and I hope you feel the same way about me."

"I do."

"Nina, I love you. I don't know how I lived before I met you. Everything has changed for me, and I hope you know that no matter what, I'm going to do everything I can to give you and our child the best life possible."

There was something strange about the way he said the last sentence, but Nina brushed it off. It felt so good to be there in his arms, sharing her feelings without worry, and knowing that he loved her as much as she loved him; maybe even more. There was something so powerful in that, and she didn't want this moment to end.

Nina was starting to drift off when Alex moved beneath her.

"We should be getting back," he said. "I have an early meeting."

Nina groaned.

"One thing you are going to have to work on before this baby comes is your work life balance. You work way too much and I'm not going to be the only one changing diapers."

"I wouldn't expect you to. Part of the reason I'm working so much now is so I won't have to work so much once the baby comes."

"If your businesses are set up properly, they should practically run themselves."

"That's what I'm hoping for."

"I can help you get there."

"You have enough on your plate." He rolled over, taking her with him so she was under him, then kissing her quickly before rolling off the bed and getting dressed. "You focus on your part of things and I'll worry about mine. What you're doing is more helpful than you realize."

He handed her clothes to her and begrudgingly, she got dressed, then followed him up to the main deck. When she started to sit down on the couch behind the captain's chair he stopped her.

"What are you doing?"

"Sitting down," she said.

"You're sitting here. If you're going to live on the water, you're going to learn to drive this thing."

She couldn't hide the child-like grin as she took the seat, listening intently as Alex explained all the controls from his spot beside her. When she finally turned on the engine and eased the yacht forward, she couldn't believe how easy it was. She guided it home, an excited thrill passing through her when she thought the word. *Home*. This was home.

The dock appeared in the distance much too soon, and when they got close, Alex moved to stand behind her, helping her guide the yacht to the dock until it was lined up perfectly. Nina almost jumped in surprise when Jaime appeared out of nowhere, securing the yacht to the dock and standing there, scowling as if he was about to lecture a couple of teenagers and not a pair of adults about to start a family.

Alex smiled at Jaime, completely unbothered by the judgement on the man's face. Alex helped Nina off the boat, then wrapped his arm around her waist, putting himself between her and Jaime.

"I'm going to walk her to her suite and I'll meet you in the office."

"It's urgent," Jaime said.

"And it will still be *urgent* in five minutes."

Jaime started to argue, thought better of it, then turned abruptly and walked away. He slunk away like an angry hulk as the sun began to set and the solar lights along the walkway started to glow where the shadows were already blocking out most of the light.

"He is very intimidating," she said.

"He's a puppy dog. It's my fault. We were supposed to be back over an hour ago."

"It was worth it," she said quietly, just in case Jaime was within earshot.

"Yes, it was."

He led her into the courtyard and through a side door, then up the back stairs to her suite.

"This is where I say goodnight," he said. "I'll be gone all day tomorrow, so don't wait for me."

He leaned in and kissed he tenderly.

"Sweet dreams, Nina."

She smiled, leaning into him, then watching him walk away before she went into her suite and closed and locked the door behind her. If Alex wouldn't be sneaking in to make love to her in the middle of the day, there was no reason to leave the door open.

She decided to call it a night, setting her alarm for early in the morning, and snuggling down in the bed until the comforter was around her chin. She had a long day ahead of her, and more than enough to do to keep her busy until Alex came home the next evening.

Closing her eyes, she started to drift off to sleep. The very last thought she had before the darkness claimed was the realization that she was *finally* going to get to drive her brand-new car.

She couldn't wait.

Chapter 12

Nina was up and at the breakfast table shortly after sunrise, but the dining room was nearly deserted. She grabbed some fruit and a couple bottles of orange juice out of the refrigerator. Her heels clicked on the marble floors as she made her way out the door.

There was a sleek, coal black car sitting in the turnabout driveway in front of the door. She recognized the mechanic instantly, though she couldn't remember his name.

"Your car, Señora," he said, handing her the keys with a huge grin on his face.

"What is this?"

"Audi A8L, security addition."

"It looks like a regular car."

His smile widened.

"Oh, but this car can withstand machine gun fire and a hand grenade."

"I don't plan on throwing either of those things at my car," she said.

The mechanic's smile slid off his face and he stared at her for a minute before her meaning dawned on him.

"Very funny."

He motioned to her to hand her phone over and she complied before she thought about it. She watched him intently as he waited patiently for the ten seconds it took to download an app, then pointed it at the car and programed it. When he tapped the screen and the engine roared to life, he smiled triumphantly.

"It's the only model with remote start," he said. "And, this button right here summons the car."

"Summons it?"

"Yep. Hit the button and make sure your GPS is on, and the car will pull right up to where you are."

"That's insane."

"It's only standard on this model, but the auto summons is supposed to be released as an option over the next couple years."

"This is an amazing car."

"And it's all yours. You have a good day. And be careful; the engine is very powerful."

She got in, setting her laptop and phone on the passenger seat and closing the door. When the door sealed, everything went silent, and she realized that the yard had been filled with the buzzing of insects in the trees, and birds calling to each other as the world awakened. The silence in the car was deafening. While she'd become accustomed to the relative silence in the cabin of luxury cars, this was far more profound.

She had no doubt that withstanding hand grenades and automatic weaponry was just the tip of the iceberg.

She eased the car onto Bayshore Lane and headed north, deciding to stop at the gas station first thing to see if her theory was right. If the bulk of the traffic was going north this morning, then the gas station should be extremely busy, which would give her a chance to see the property in action.

It would take a little longer to go through the new software with their cash office clerk since they also took care of customers at the gas station, but she was willing to take that chance. Seeing the business running at capacity might give her a better feel for the business as a whole, and once she had everyone working through the new system, she would be able to generate reports that Alex could use to streamline his business.

She was starting to feel giddy as the possibilities ran through her mind. It was all so exciting, and she couldn't wait to see how her expertise lent itself to improving the overall business model and making Alex more money. He was going to be thrilled.

She fought her way through the heavy traffic, the sleek car turning heads as she maneuvered down the 395. She took the exit when her phone prompted her and pulled into the familiar gas station.

It was completely empty.

Maybe it's just a lull, she thought, parking next to the employee's car on the side, just in case the station suddenly got busy. When she entered the store it was equally quiet, and the clerk didn't appear for quite some time after the doorbell chimed to announce her presence.

"The pumps are broken and—" the man was saying as he walked down the aisle, then stopped abruptly when he saw her. "Miss Nina, I didn't know you were coming today. Is everything alright?"

"Just came to walk you through the new accounting system."

"I'm sure I can manage," he said warmly.

His obvious dismissal irritated her.

"There are certain aspects that are completely different from the old software. Part of my job is to make sure that everyone has inputted their information correctly so the process is smooth. It's not about what your location does anymore, it's about the whole business. Surely, you can understand why making sure we're all on the same page is important."

He looked like he was going to argue, but she stood her ground, crossing her arms and raising a single eyebrow in challenge. The man stared at her for a second, as if he couldn't believe that she was for real, then his shoulders slumped ever so slightly and he motioned with his head toward the cash office in the back.

"Let's get this over with so I can get back to work," he grumbled.

"Aren't you going to lock the front door so we don't get robbed blind while we're in there?"

Her question caught him off guard, then he nodded and did as she asked.

Nina shook her head, using her phone to make a note that would sync automatically with the files on her laptop. This note was for her eyes only, and she quickly wrote down the manager's complete lack of common sense and poor work ethic, then made a note that the store should be audited for shrinkage.

She had a feeling more merchandise was stolen from this store than purchased.

She followed the man to the office, taking out her laptop and setting it on the rickety table they were using as a desk.

"Where is the computer that's supposed to be in here?"

"We use a laptop."

"Alright, but where is it? I can't really show you how to do this without the computer in front of you."

"Aren't we just using the old software?"

She sighed.

"Look, I'm not going to look at your browser history, so whatever you were looking at before I walked in, I don't care. It's up to you whether you dick around all day on the internet of get some actual work done, because as the store manager, any dip in profits come down on you. So, whatever it is you're trying to hide, I'm not even looking for.

I'm uploading the updated version of the software, syncing the old files with the new software, and showing you how to input new information. I'm trying to do all twenty-two properties this week, and you're slowing me down. I'm not here to play games, I'm here to get stuff done. So, please, get the laptop, shut down whatever you were looking at and then bring it here so I can update everything and be on my way. You can waste *your* time, but I'm not about to let you waste mine."

Her words must have had some effect on him, because he finally quit arguing and left the room, coming back almost five minutes later with the laptop in hand, giving it to her after unlocking it with the password.

Updating the software while they spoke, she gave him a quick rundown of how the new system worked, including the features she was most excited about. As she went through the list and the software finished loading, she synced the old program with the new, then went into the settings menu and scrolled down until she found what she was looking for.

She found the single credit card machine on the dropdown menu, right-clicking on it and pairing it with the laptop.

"There, now you won't have to come to the cash register unless there's a customer."

"Okay?" he said, clearly confused.

She clicked on the icon again, then ran the reports. It generated a saved file almost instantly, naming it the current date and time.

"You'll have to run reports again tonight, but I wanted to show you how it works. You choose *run reports*, then when this little file pops up, you drag it to this area right here, and drop it. It automatically inputs your reports and updates the file. It's probably the easiest thing you'll do all day, and that's saying a lot."

"I don't have to do anything else?"

"You will have to count the cash drawer and note any discrepancies, but otherwise, the system does most of the work for you."

She checked her laptop, making sure that the information synced in real time as it was supposed to, thrilled to find that everything she'd done on his laptop was already on hers.

It worked exactly how she thought it would, and she was delighted. This was going to make keeping track of twenty-two separate businesses doable. Alex was going to be so happy when he saw what she'd done, and how she'd taken initiative. Everything was already looking better, and by the end of the week, she would have every penny Alex spent and earned at her fingertips. Only then would she show him what she'd managed to do, and she hoped that he was surprised.

    She set her computer to sleep and packed it up, thanked the manager, then followed him to the door so he could let her out. The parking lot was still empty, though traffic on the freeway was still packed. She'd been there long enough that there should have been several customers, but there hadn't been a single customer. It was weird, but she'd only been there about an hour, so it was possible that she'd just found a lull in an otherwise steady day.

If not, and this was par for the course, the reports she would generate every quarter would make it clear that the gas station was not making the money it should, and Alex would likely sell the place if he didn't want to deal with the hassle of making necessary changes. Either way, she'd be making a difference, and that made her feel like she was doing more than just crunching numbers to justify her allowance. She was earning her salary and it felt good.

    The morning air was already warm when she stepped onto the walkway that led around the side of the building to her car. She almost thought she heard the manager lock the door behind her, but he was probably just removing the key. Dead or not, there was no way he was going to just lock the doors and give up for the day before it was even eight in the morning. The store manager didn't strike her as the brightest star in the sky, but no one was that stupid.

She looked at the map of properties, picking the next one down the line. She'd already broken them up into mini territories, so each day she would visit between four and six properties, depending on how close they were to the others. Today, she was hitting a cluster of six, then heading home to go through the files and make sure she'd worked out all the kinks before doing it again the next day. Even though the gas station manager had dragged the twenty-minute process out being difficult, the next five properties were all within a few minutes of each other, and she would finish before lunch. Her first paycheck had already hit her bank, so she would treat herself to a nice, early lunch out for a change, then finish her workday in her office. By the time she was done for the day, it would still be early, and she could take a swim and relax until Alex came home.

The next five properties went just like she expected, and unlike the lazy store manager at the gas station, the clerks greeted her with warm smiles, ready to learn about the new system, and interested in how it was going to make everything run smoother. She was in and out of each property in less than thirty minutes, and as she expected, she was done well before lunch. At this rate, she would have everyone on the same page by Friday, which was exciting.

You're such a nerd, she thought, still laughing. But she loved what she did, and a position like this was almost unheard of for someone fresh out of college. What could have been the biggest mistake of her life had turned out to be so much better than she could have imagined. She had a great car, a well-paying job that she could use as a stepping stone to a lucrative career, a baby on the way, and a good man that really got her like no one else ever had.

Nina couldn't have planned a better life for herself, and she couldn't wait to see Alex tonight to tell him everything she'd accomplished. Life was good.

Chapter 13

Nina stepped out of the shower, toweling her straight hair dry as she stood in front of her closet and tried to decide what to wear. It was almost five, and she had enjoyed a good swim, finished her work for the day, and her day was done. She had already reviewed the properties she'd visited that day and merged them with her Masterfile. Everything was working exactly as it should, and when she'd checked the point of sale hardware for each property, they were still synced in real time and available for Nina.

This time next month, she would only be making property visits for random audits, making sure that the employees knew that there would be accountability and Nina wasn't just going to assume that the computer-generated reports were correct. They were accurate, and almost instant, but that didn't mean they couldn't be affected by human error or design. Even the most sophisticated systems could be breeched and Nina knew that being subject to random audits was a huge deterrent.

Alex had called right before she'd showered to let her know he wouldn't make dinner and not to wait up for him, just in case. She usually wore something cute to dinner, but tonight, she was thinking simple and comfortable. Skipping over the sweatpants and opting for her favorite pair of jeans, Nina paired them with a loose-fitting tee and a pair of athletic shoes with just a hint of pink.

When she turned to check herself out in the full-length mirror, she couldn't believe how different she looked. It wasn't just the fact that she was starting to get a baby bump, though this was probably the last time she could comfortably wear these jeans. She could see the change in herself, and it wasn't just physical. She was confident, and the stress of making grades and wondering what her future held was gone.

She couldn't remember ever being this content with her life, even though she'd always been a very happy, positive person. This was different. It came from a life without surprises, where everyone was assured everything they needed and more. Their child would never know the stress of parents sitting at the table until the early hours of the morning, trying to squeeze another dollar out of what they had left, yet somehow making it work.

Her baby would never skip high school parties in favor of extra credit that would ensure another scholarship. Nina had worked so hard in high school that her college was paid for entirely through scholarships, including a monthly stipend for necessities and a meal plan. She had even won a scholarship that had paid for her textbooks and laptop. But she had given up so much of her childhood for those things. She would never regret it but knowing that her child wouldn't have to do the same felt good.

That profound security and contentment was written all over her face.

Pulling herself away from the mirror and all that soul-searching, Nina looked at the clock and decided she had time to check the six accounts from today one more time. It was five, and they would be running at each of the properties even though Nina had run them once today. There was a five to ten second delay on each report, but that was nothing. If she hurried and everyone did their job, she could do a quick reports audit and make any necessary tweaks before dinner.

Excited, she fired up the laptop on her desk and logged into the system. As she expected, two of the properties had already begun to manually upload their reports from the point of sale, creating a new file for Nina to approve before it was merged with the Masterfile.

Surprisingly, the gas station had already run its reports and they were ready for her to review. She clicked on the file, opening it up and staring at it, dumbfounded.

The gas station had pulled in a couple grand in sales in just a few hours.

"Maybe this morning was a fluke," she said out loud, shocked that any place that could be so dead during peak hours could still more than make up for it in the middle of the day.

She saved the file, leaving the merging for later. She was eager to see how the other properties had faired throughout the day, and merging the files took a bit of time, so it was better to merge them all at once at the end.

The next property was one of the larger hotels, and it was no surprise that they'd done over a million dollars in business since she'd been there. The clerks had been extremely busy the entire time she'd been there, and only the cash office clerk had been free long enough to watch her use the system. Even then, he'd been distracted and obviously ready for her to leave so he could go out and help the others. Like Fontainebleau, this hotel was right on the water, and there was really no "off-season." With the summer looming, it was only going to get busier.

She saved the file with the name of the hotel and the date, then moved onto the next one. This one was the small one that she and Alex gone to first. Like the week before, she hadn't seen a single customer at the desk to check in, and the hotel lacked the constant bustling of smaller hotels. She was pretty sure it was completely empty, at least on the first floor.

The report had just been pulled from two out of the three points of sale she'd synced with their computer. She watched as the third one began to upload its numbers, then opened the file before the clerk had even saved it. It wouldn't affect the clerk on her end, and she wouldn't be able to see that Nina was in the file. That was one of the perks of the system she had left out. Alex's cash office staff didn't need to know that she had unfettered access to everything, and she could pull a screen shot from the file in real time if she needed to, in addition to the screen shots the program did automatically.

Everything had been created with high-volume sales in mind, which kept people from skimming a few hundred here and there, thinking that it would never be missed amongst the millions. If Alex hired anyone who turned out to be a thief, Nina would be the first to know.

The report loaded, and Nina found herself shocked yet again. The hotel had cleared an astounding amount of money for its size, and it had been the last property on Nina's round that day. How it made even a tenth of that in just 5 hours was beyond her, but the amount they made would have raised a brow even in a full day's report.

"Those are some expensive ass rooms," she said, opening the web browser and typing the hotel name into the search bar.

It took her forever to find the property, and once she did, she discovered that the physical address was wrong. Really wrong. She wasn't even sure if the street it was listed on existed in downtown Miami. But the phone numbers matched the ones she'd saved to the file, and the pictures of the property were correct.

Furrowing her brow, she clicked through the site until she found the place to make reservations, which wasn't readily available on the main menu. When she pulled up the prices and pictures of the individual rooms, she couldn't believe that a regular hotel room cost that much. It was almost five hundred dollars a night for a one-bedroom suite with a kitchenette.

Nina was floored. There was no way this location warranted that price. Opening another tab on the browser, she searched hotels in the vicinity, using the correct address as a starting point. There were five hotels within two miles of Alex's hotel, some of them in much better locations. And all of them were under two hundred a night.

"What the hell?" she said, thinking back to the outrageous price the gas station was charging for a gallon of gas compared to the place across the highway.

How were any of these places staying afloat?

Curious, and feeling a little uneasy, Nina tried to book a room, but there was a glitch on the website that wouldn't allow her to book. She called the number on the website, setting her own number to *private* before she dialed by pushing *67 first.

Her call was answered on the first ring.

"Mirada Extended Stay, how can I help you?" a cheery voice answered.

"I'm trying to book a room but your website isn't working. And I have a couple questions about the amenities."

"Confirmation code?"

"What?"

"Do you have a booking confirmation code?"

"I couldn't book a room, that's why I'm calling."

"I'm sorry, there are no vacancies at this time."

"Are you sure?" she challenged, but the line went dead in her ear.

"What the hell," she muttered.

This wasn't adding up. Neither were the sales at the gas station. They were in line with the success of Fontainebleau, but these two businesses should have been in the red or close to it. Something was wrong.

Nina looked up the specs on the hotel, coming up with a consistent eighty-five rooms total. That made sense, since there were three floors and each floor had about twenty-six rooms. Double-checking her math with her calculator, she came up with a max sales amount of just under forty-three thousand dollars a day. That was if they sold every room at the max price and were at capacity, which she was sure they weren't.

But their sales for the day were nearly double that, and the number of rooms sold was listed at almost two hundred. According to the reported sales at Mirada, there were more rooms booked than existed on the property.

Her stomach dropped and her hand shook as she used the computer mouse to copy the file and save it to the desktop. Alex needed to see this, and he wasn't going to be happy. But she had two more properties to check, and she didn't want to make any conclusions until she saw the others.

She pulled the last two reports, her heart racing when she found much of the same. The first report was similar to Mirada and the gas station, but it was the final one that really caught her attention. Unlike the three that were doing so much more business than what Nina had seen with her own eyes, *this* property was pulling in almost nothing.

It was one of those entertainment centers people loved to drop their teens and tweens at, with a roller skating rink, batting cage, more arcade games than she'd ever seen in one place in her life, a four-lane bowling alley and laser tag. There were also two concession stands that served pizza, hotdogs, hamburgers and drinks.

Throughout the massive building, there were change-making machines to change dollars into quarters for the arcade games, but most of the kids had wristbands with barcodes that they could scan at each activity. A ticket was only good for two hours, and no one under the age of eighteen could exit without an adult checking them out.

The place had been packed, the cash office way in the back of the building. Nina had been overwhelmed by all the noise and kids running around, burning off their energy now that they were out of school. That place should have grossed at least five thousand just in entrance fees during each two-hour period, but it had barely cleared five thousand over the past seven hours. That wasn't counting all the food, paid games, equipment rental and everything else. She had seen the platinum wristband, which was almost two hundred for unlimited food and play, on most of the kids there.

It had seemed like a lot, but when she thought about how much the kids were eating and playing, and the fact that included the entrance fee and meant that frazzled parents could get a break for two hours without worrying about their child leaving the venue, it really wasn't that much. In the affluent location, with all the expensive cars in the parking lot during pick up and drop off, Nina knew that was a drop in the bucket to most of these parents, and the kids probably went several times a week.

This business should have been a cash cow, but it was a financial dud. There was no way the reports matched up with reality.

Now she knew something was wrong.

She looked through the reports she'd pulled that morning. Simply going through the motions to show the clerks how to work the new system, she hadn't paid much attention to the particulars. Now, it seemed much more important. With each file she pulled up, she found more of the same. Mirada, the gas station off the 395, and the entertainment hall were showing similarly skewed numbers.

The other businesses were showing sales that made sense, and profits that were in line with their overhead. It was just the three properties that were filling Nina's head with alarm bells. They accounted for fifty percent of her day. What if the numbers ran the same with the other businesses? Would half of the twenty-two come up skewed? How long had this been going on, and did Alex know he was being robbed?

Her phone chimed, making her jump.

"Not now," she grumbled, snoozing the Spanish app reminder she'd set, thinking she would have plenty of time each night around this time.

She had bigger things to deal with.

She was putting her phone in her pocket when she stopped, remembering the conversation the two clerks had while she'd been waiting for the program to sync with all the different points of sale in the hotel.

They'd had the conversation entirely in Spanish even though they both spoke perfect English. At the time, she'd been so focused on what she was doing that she hadn't minded. It kept her from getting sucked into the conversation while she was trying to focus. Now, she wondered if they'd said something they didn't want her to understand.

Hands shaking, she opened the app, scrolling through the random recording the app had picked up at dinner and throughout her day. When she finally found the short recording from today right before lunch, she hit *play* and watched the video load, her heart racing.

"Is this really a good idea?"

"He knows what he's doing. If the feds come after him, the numbers will prove that nothing is going on."

"But what about the woman? What if she finds out?"

"It doesn't matter. He's a billionaire and she's pregnant with his child. She's not going to risk ruining that."

"Did you take unit five offline?"

"Yes. We'll use that for the rest and keep one through four clean."

"Do you think that will be enough?"

Nina's voice interrupted them then, and the recording stopped abruptly, but she'd heard enough. It was clear that Alex was aware of the discrepancies, and that it was intentional. He was using his businesses to launder money and probably had been for years.

She added up everything, including what she estimated the entertainment hall should have made during its business hours. The number she was left with was staggering, and she knew she'd only just scratched the surface. It seemed that her business savvy billionaire was making mounds of money the easy way. By cheating the system. If the IRS caught him, he was going down and taking her with him.

She couldn't let that happen, even if she had to confront him about it and give him an ultimatum. He was already staggeringly wealthy, playing by the rules wouldn't hurt him. If she could appeal to his protective instincts over herself and their baby, maybe she could convince him to fly clean from now on.

But she was going to need more ammo to convince him that she knew everything, and a few skewed reports from a small sampling of his properties wasn't going to cut it. She needed more, and she knew where to find it.

Checking the time, she was glad to see that dinner was getting started. The guards would be distracted, timing their meals so that everyone had a chance to eat without the mansion being vulnerable. This was the perfect time to do a little sneaking around.

But what if Alex came home while she was snooping?

She decided to prevent that, texting him quickly and getting a response back almost immediately.

I miss you, she wrote.

I'll be home around 8, he responded.

Good. She had almost two hours, and she didn't need half that. Grabbing a flash drive out of her drawer, she left her room, heading to the forbidden office on the first floor. She was going to get to the bottom of this, and then she would confront him. How he ran his business before they met was his business. Now that she was in charge of his books and risking her freedom if he was ever caught, it was hers.

Chapter 14

The office was dark, the door locked with a key. But Nina was prepared for that. After walking boldly into Alex's room, which she was allowed to do anyway, she'd retrieved the key-ring she'd seen in his desk drawer when she'd surprised him with lunch in his suite one day while he was working. He'd managed to be nonchalant about shutting the drawer quickly, but not before she'd gotten a glimpse of most of what was in there. At the time, she'd thought he was protecting her from seeing the handgun that was mounted on the sidewall of the drawer, but now she wasn't so sure. There had been quite a few things in the drawer that could be sketchy now that she knew Alex was evading taxes. But she would worry about those things after she hit the downstairs office. She knew from her forensic accounting class that what she was looking for would be out of sight and not easily accessed, and the most logical place was the locked office.

She looked down the hall, thankful that the layout of the house provided her cover from the front doors and the main staircase. Someone would have to be coming down the hall to see her, and the dining room, which was at the end of the west hallway, was still filled with laughter and boisterous conversation that could be heard from the east hallway.

No one would be coming down this hall anytime soon, and the only access to the formal dining room was the west hallway, so staff coming and going wouldn't be anywhere near where she was. And the rest of the staff would be patrolling the ground until they were relieved for their turn at dinner.

It took trying three keys before the lock finally turned, and she quickly slipped into the room, locking the door behind her just in case. She stood in the darkness for a moment, letting her eyes become accustomed to the low light. It was twilight outside, but this office had both heavy blinds and thick curtains that kept almost all the lights out.

Now that she knew that Alex was likely hiding some of his financial information, it made sense that the room would seem especially fortified. Even people who felt justified in skirting the law were paranoid about it.

When she could see well enough not to bump into anything, she made her way through the large room. The computer was on the desk, already on and running with the standard screen saver bouncing along the edges of the screen.

The heavy desk had several drawers, all of them locked with a key. She probably had the key on the keyring, but she didn't really care about what was in the drawers right then. If she had time when she was done breaking into the computer, she would worry about the drawers.

She tapped the keyboard, and the password prompt appeared. She tried a few options that were similar to the passcodes from the properties, but nothing worked. She'd broken into the office for nothing, and now she had to figure out how to leave, still with nothing to show for her efforts. Angry, she glared at the computer, hitting *enter* one last time, even though she hadn't typed anything yet.

A dialog box appeared, asking if she would like to retrieve the password by answering a security question. She almost clicked *cancel*, then decided to give it a try. The worst thing that would happen was she would find out that she knew nothing about Alex. Since discovering the tax evasion, she already knew that she didn't know nearly enough, so it wouldn't be a shock to find that she had no inkling of his most privileged information. Or the question could be something simple, like the make and model of Alex's car, or the type of yacht he owned. Those were questions she could answer in her sleep.

"It couldn't be that easy," she mumbled, clicking *OK* and waiting for the question to appear.

She didn't expect much, so when the question appeared, and it wasn't completely foreign to her, she almost whooped with delight.

What color was the house on 23rd Street? the question read.

She stared at the screen, wracking her brain. She *knew* this, but her mind instantly drew a blank. Alex had told her this when he was talking about his childhood, and she had thought it was odd he'd even mentioned the color of his house.

But she'd brushed it off. People often remembered the most off-the-wall things from their childhood, so it made sense that his mind might hold onto such an inconsequential fact. She'd been in grade school when her grandmother passed away and had no recollection of the woman beyond the fact that she always wore purple shoes. The mind was a funny thing, but this childhood memory was one Alex had freely shared with her.

Maybe he wasn't being as secretive with his life as she'd thought.

She ran through a few colors in her mind before it finally hit her.

"Peach!" she whispered excitedly, typing the answer, then taking a picture of the password with her phone's camera when it appeared on the screen.

It was a series of random numbers and letters, and she never would have guessed the actual password in a million years. She used the right-click on the mouse to copy the password, then pasted it on the sign-on screen. Still afraid it wasn't going to work, she held her breath as the computer finally loaded everything up.

She plugged the flash drive into the USB port, copying every folder on the desktop one at a time without looking at the contents. She would look at the files later, when she wasn't pushing her luck by being in the office when she knew she wasn't supposed to be.

When she'd copied all but the last folder, she heard someone in the hall and froze.

Keep walking, she urged silently, but the footsteps on the tile floors had already stopped, and she could see someone's shadow pass in front of the light that seeped in through the gap in the door.

Shit! Nina thought, ejecting the flash drive as soon as the file was uploaded and shoving the thumb drive into the top of her shoe. She logged off the computer as the key slipped into the lock, looking for a place to hide, then deciding against it. She wasn't going to get out of here if she was trapped behind a curtain like some ridiculous spy movie. She had one chance to pull it off, and she was going to own it.

She jumped onto the couch as the handle turned and threw her arm over her face, letting her body go limp like she was asleep.

The door opened and the light turned on, and Nina jumped as if she'd been startled out of a deep sleep, blinking at the doorway as if in confusion.

"What are you doing in here?" a familiar voice hissed from the doorway.

It was Jaime.

"I was coming down to dinner and I felt sick. I needed somewhere to lay down and I guess I dozed off."

Had the screen saver popped up yet? Nina wondered frantically, glad the monitor was turned so its back was to the office door. Hopefully, it would engage before Jaime tired of talking to her, and he wouldn't know she'd been on the computer at all.

"You're not supposed to be in here," he grumbled.

"It was the first door I came to. I thought it was a bathroom. This house is really big and maybe *you* know it like the back of your hand, but I still get turned around in the garden. The inside of the house feels like a giant maze sometimes."

She glared at him, daring him to call her a liar. *He* might be the boss's number one, but Nina was carrying Alex's child. Jaime didn't compare to her place in Alex's life and they both knew it. Would he stand his ground long enough, or would his suspicious nature take over and call her bluff?

"I'm not buying it," Jaime said, bluntly. "You're up to something."

"You're paranoid," she shot back. "I'm pregnant, I got lightheaded and a little dizzy, and I laid down. Stop trying to make a rivalry between us a thing. Alex is still your friend, and this is not a competition. We're not even on the same level."

Jaime scoffed and she knew she'd hit the nail on the head. He was threatened by her presence, and that was making him paranoid. That had to be it.

"Look, Jamie," she said, purposefully mispronouncing his name.

"It's *Jaime*."

"Whatever. Is dinner ready? Do you think you can walk me to the dining room so I don't pass out before I eat? I think my sugar was low and I need to eat."

"No," he said flatly. "If you can find your way into places that you aren't welcome, you can make it to the dining room. How did you get in here without a key?"

"The door was ajar. I guess you didn't lock it properly. It was pretty dark in the room with the blinds and these heavy curtains, and I saw a couch. I didn't even turn on the light to look around, and I guess I didn't realize that the door knob was locked when I kicked it closed. Good thing I didn't need help from someone who might actually help me. They would have had to kick down the door."

Jaime came closer, and Nina fought the urge to panic. If she looked guilty now, he would be even more suspicious. She couldn't risk that.

"I don't know what you're up to," he said, his voice low and menacing. "But you better not ruin this for me. Stay out of this office and watch yourself. You're playing with fire, and Alex isn't going to tolerate your shit just because you're carrying his baby. He's thrown trash out of this house for less."

Nina nearly shot up, itching to slap the smug look off his face and make him sorry he ever called her trash, but she knew he was trying to trick her. She scowled instead, sitting up slowly and putting her hands on either side of her like she needed extra support when really, she need something to grab to keep her from scratching his eyes out for what he'd said.

"It's obvious that you have some personal baggage," she said. "I have to get something to eat, and I'm not going to sit here and take your shit. You need to get right with yourself before you go judging others."

"I don't care what you think of me. Keep your nose out of our business and stay out of this room, am I clear?"

His tone chaffed, but she smiled instead of scowling, which she could tell instantly got under his skin.

"Crystal clear," she said, standing and walking right by him as if she had no fear.

The truth was, she was trembling, and the rigid drive in her shoe pinched her with each step. She was careful, walking so she didn't risk breaking the drive. Jaime followed her to the door, locking it behind her loudly.

As soon as she was in the stairwell, she pulled the drive out of her shoe, shoved it in her pocket and all but ran up the stairs. She had no way of knowing if the screen saver had come on while they were talking, and if Jaime came after her, she wanted a head start locking herself in her room.

Jaime never came after her, but she locked the main door to her suite anyway, then took her laptop to the bedroom and locked that door, too. The office was the only room that didn't have balcony access, and if she ended up trapped in this room with Jaime on the other side, she wanted some way of escaping.

This was between her and Alex, and even if Jaime was in on it, she wasn't involving him. She needed to see what was on the flash drive and decide what she was going to do. She was either going to leave, or she was going to give him the chance to fly right. There was no other option.

She loaded the flash drive and sighed when it automatically started syncing with her accounting program. She should have turned the auto-sync off before she plugged the drive in, but she couldn't stop it now.

Once it was loaded, synced and organized by her software, she started opening files and skimming the content. Some of them seemed innocent enough, but it was the last file that had waded into something much bigger than she realized.

The latest bank statements for business accounts at banks she didn't recognize. It was a lot of money. An almost impossible amount.

She clicked through each file, the picture becoming clearer with each new piece of information. With a sinking heart, she realized that Alex wasn't just evading taxes. Alex was using his business to launder money in outrageously large sums. Which is why he needed luxury hotels and not just a handful of little hotels like Mirada.

He was moving small enough amounts from each property's account to these offshore accounts that the US banks wouldn't bat an eye at the transfers without the whole picture. Just under ten thousand per business didn't seem like much, but multiplied by twenty-two, meant that almost two hundred thousand a *day* was being moved.

Laundering that amount of money could only mean one thing.

Alex was part of a drug cartel, and he was using these businesses to launder money to hide it from the government.

Suddenly, it all made sense. The guards, the nice house that was secluded in the middle of the city. The hotel that required a password to book a room probably catered to businessmen who needed a safe place to party, which explained the insane price of the rooms. It was probably by the hour.

And the gas station? There were infinite possibilities, and being that close to a major highway, they weren't good. Alex was in deep, and Nina realized in that moment that he wasn't just part of a cartel. He had to be one of its leaders, or pretty high up. There was no way he had the amount of money he did without being someone very important in the cartel. A simple ultimatum wasn't going to work.

She was going to have to come up with something much more compelling, and she was going to have to stand her ground. She didn't know how Alex had gotten wrapped up in something like this, but she knew he was a good guy, and even more important, she knew that he loved her. He wasn't going to let her walk away, and she definitely wasn't going to raise a child in this kind of life.

*

Nina was still sitting on her bed, trying to figure out what to say, when a text from Alex came through her phone.

Your door is locked, it read. She shoved it in her pocket, steeling herself for a confrontation she knew would *not* be pretty.

She opened the bedroom door, then opened the suite door and let him in, stomach in knots, mind racing. She locked the door behind him and sat in the chair, gesturing for him to sit across from her.

"It must be serious," he said, sitting down. "Are you okay? Is the baby okay?"

"The baby is fine, but I'm not okay, Alex. We need to talk."

He took a slow, deep breath.

"Actually, that's why I'm here right now. I have something I need to talk to you about, but I had to tie up a few loose ends first."

"I need to go first," she said. "If I don't say it now, I'm going to lose my nerve."

"Alright, what's on your mind."

He leaned forward and reached out to hold her hands in his, but she ignored the gesture and he just sat there, waiting for her to find the words.

"I know, Alex."

"At the risk of sounding like an ass, what do you know?"

"Everything."

"I don't know how you could know everything, but I'll bite. What is everything?"

"Stop playing with me. I updated your software, and the new system is more connected than in the past. I can check the points of sale in real time, retrieve cash office files directly from my computer without the properties knowing, and I can see every transaction that happens throughout the day, all from my laptop."

He sucked in a quick breath.

"I didn't know there were accounting programs that did that."

"It's a program my college professor created. I helped him work on it and I still had it on my laptop. It's still in the testing stages, but it works exactly like it's supposed to. And I found something."

"What did you find?"

"I think you know."

"We both know that I know," he countered. "But what I need from you is to know what exactly you found so I know what to say."

"I'm not going to let this go, Alex."

"I don't expect you to."

"Then, why not just tell me everything?"

"Everything is a lot, Nina."

"I gathered that." She sighed, looking down at her hands for a moment and wishing that this day would come to an end. "This is more uncomfortable than I thought. Look, I know you're a good guy, Alex. But good people do bad things for money. I know you're laundering money for a drug cartel."

When she looked at him, he didn't look appalled. She knew that she was right, and her heart broke in that instant. She hadn't wanted it to be true, but it obviously was.

"I'm not going to insult your intelligence by denying it," he said after a brief silence. "I started working for the drug cartel when I was a teenager. My stepdad brought me into the family business."

"Does the cartel own all those properties? The house? The cars?"

"No," he said, almost chuckling. "Believe it or not, I saved my money and worked my ass off, and when I got the life insurance from my parents, I took that money and invested in my first property. Every dime I made, I reinvested until I had more than I knew what to do with."

"That's smart."

"It is. My stepdad wanted out for years after he met my mom, but he never had enough money to buy his freedom. When he died, I picked up where he left off, but I did it knowing I wouldn't do it forever. They took everything he had, but he showed me how to play the system."

"The offshore accounts."

This statement actually earned a look of surprise from Alex.

"You've got some nerve." He laughed. "Man, this kid is going to be the death of me if he's anything like you."

"And if it's a girl?"

"I'm in more trouble than I know how to handle."

This time when he tried to take her hands, she didn't pull away. She looked into his eyes, searching for the man she knew he was, and trying to reconcile that with the stereotypical cartel employee. She couldn't see it.

"Do you run the cartel?"

"No. Not even close. I'm one of the higherups, but I still have to work for a living. When they saw how well my investments were doing, they saw an opportunity to use my good name and reputation for something more. It came with a pay raise, my own guards and the lifestyle I'd always wanted. I finally didn't have to hide what I had, because they expected me to live like this. It's part of my cover, and as long as they see the money they expect to see, there are no issues."

"What are you going to do now?"

"It's already done," he said. "Carlos wasn't happy, but he understood. A lot of men get out when they start a family. You can't imagine what rival cartels do to families."

Nina felt sick. She hadn't considered that.

"I arranged to buy out tonight, and Carlos accepted my offer. I know you love this house, but I think it's best if we move somewhere else."

"Away from Miami?"

"No. Just not this house. You can keep the car, though. I bought that with clean money. And I still want you to manage accounting for my properties, but I'll only have fifteen."

"I can guess which ones you're letting go of."

"The ones they were using to launder money. I'll transfer them to an umbrella corporation, so they still appear to be in my name and don't draw attention, but as of tomorrow, everything will be done, and I've asked them to have Jaime take my place."

"At least he'll be happy about something."

"Jaime is a good guy. If you give him a chance, you'll see that."

"He called me trash."

"I'll talk to him. That isn't going to fly."

"So, we're just moving and getting a new place?"

"If you'll come with me. I understand if that's hard for you to do."

"All I want is for you to give up this life so we can raise our child better than you were." She shook her head. "I'm sorry, that came out wrong."

"I know what you mean. It's not that simple, but I'm taking steps to make sure we can walk away and I—"

The house shook and the lights flashed, then went off, the room pitch black in an instant.

"What was that?" Nina asked, but Alex already had her by the hand, dragging her toward the door that led to the balcony.

"DEA," he hissed. "Follow me."

She did as she was told, running onto the balcony just as gunfire erupted and men started shouting.

Alex vaulted over the railing, hung for a second, then dropped silently into the garden.

He stood beneath where she was, holding his hands out and motioning to her. She was shaking her head when there was another explosion, this time closer, and more gunfire. Men were shouting and running from the carriage house, and she didn't have time to be afraid.

She climbed over the rail, lowered herself as far as she could, then jumped. Alex's strong arms grabbed her, softening her fall so the landing wasn't so jarring. Before she could catch her breath, they were on the move again, heading straight for the dock. Alex pushed her ahead of him, pulling a gun and returning fire when the bullets started flying their way. She heard Alex grunt, but he kept running.

A shadow appeared on their right, heading in the same direction. Nina prepared for the impact of bullets, but the figure wasn't aiming in their direction. When he made it to the gate ahead of her and punched in the code, Nina almost cried out in relief when she recognized Jaime.

"Come on," he urged, closing the gate behind Alex and running down the dock behind them.

Nina didn't wait for Alex to help, leaping onto the yacht and running to the helm. Alex and Jaime had the ropes untied by the time Nina got the engine fired up, men shouting in Spanish already getting closer.

"Go, go, go!" Jaime yelled, and Nina gunned it, heading north as fast as she dared.

Alex sat down on the chair across from her, his breath coming in heavy gasps while Jaime rummaged around in a box that Nina quickly realized was a first aid kit.

"Are you shot?" Nina asked.

"It went through," Alex said, his voice calm. "I'll be fine, Jaime just needs to clean the wound."

"Oh my god, Alex! You've been shot! Why wouldn't they just arrest us instead?"

"That wasn't the feds," Jaime said, cleaning Alex's wound while Alex gritted his teeth against the pain. "That was *Mal Hombres*. A rival cartel."

"No, it wasn't," Alex corrected. "It was our people, *Cienfuegos*. I should have known it couldn't be that easy."

"What do you mean?"

"I bought them out."

"You quit?"

"I had to. This isn't a life, Jaime. At least, not one for a family. I told them you would be the best replacement."

Jaime was speechless, still cleaning and dressing the wound.

"You're one of my best men, Jaime. You *are* the best, and you're like a brother to me. I knew you would be the right man for the job."

"What do we do now?" Nina asked.

"I turn myself in and make a deal, I guess," Alex said. "I need to talk to my lawyer and—"

The sound of a gun cocking stopped him midsentence.

"I'm not going to let you do that," Jaime said, his voice cold. "I did not give up everything so you could turn yourself in."

"If you want to work for them, then fine, Jaime. Go for it. Your name won't cross my lips. But, if you think they're going to welcome you with open arms after tonight, you're wrong. Any of my men that got away will be looking over their shoulders for the rest of their lives. Carlos decides who lives and who dies, and it looks like he made his choice."

"That's not what this is about."

"Then what is it about?"

"If you turn yourself in, everything I've done will be for nothing. I'm not willing to give this up without a fight. You're as good as dead to me if you do that."

"Jaime, you're not making any sense."

"Don't you think it was a little too convenient that I hired on as a bouncer right before you bought the club? And what about growing up in your hood? Come on, Alex, don't make me spell it out. I was the perfect man for the job because being the perfect man *is* my job."

"What the hell are you talking about?" Nina said, staring at Jaime. "You're not making any sense."

But Alex knew exactly what was going on, and he looked devastated.

"We were friends for five years, Jaime. You've been with me longer than anyone. How could you do this?"

"Do what?" Nina asked, frustrated.

But it was Alex, not Jaime, who answered.

"He's undercover, Nina. Jaime is DEA."

"You've got to be shitting me," Nina said. "All this time you were acting like I was sticking my nose where it doesn't belong and we were practically on the same side?"

"I was worried you would blow my case."

"Why didn't you just say that?"

"Would you have kept that from Alex?"

"Probably not."

"Then, that's why I didn't say anything. Men get killed for being suspected of being an agent. My life wasn't worth telling you."

"Put the gun away, Jaime."

"No. You're under arrest, and as soon as we get to land, I'm going to dispatch agents to clean up that mess at your house and gather evidence." He turned and looked at Nina, who was still steering the boat north. "You don't have to worry, you can testify against Alex and save yourself. They won't try you, anyway. You've only been here a few weeks and only just found out, so you're safe."

"I won't testify against him."

Both men stared at her in shock, but Alex smiled.

"I have enough to nail you both for laundering and fraud. If you don't testify, you're screwed."

"That's a chance I'll have to—"

There was another explosion, causing all three to jump. A fireball sailed into the air, then disappeared as another explosion rocked the neighborhood. Alex turned to Jaime and smiled.

"Looks like your evidence just went up in smoke. Put the gun away and we'll figure this out. If you can keep me out of jail, I have no problem giving you all the credit for bringing me in."

"Alex, what if he's lying?"

"We don't have many options, Nina, and it looks like Carlos was serious about getting rid of every trace of my existence."

"You're going to need protection," Jaime added, holstering the gun and going back to work bandaging the wound.

"So, that's it? You're just going to forgive him for pulling a gun on you and lying to you for five years?"

"What choice do we have, Nina? I don't want to go to jail, and I'll be damned if you do. We have information that isn't available anywhere else, and the DEA needs us to get to the bigger fish."

"I don't know about this, Alex."

"It's going to be okay. Trust me."

"We need to get to shore and find a way to get to the office," Jaime said.

"It's not like we can call an Uber." Alex laughed. "Maybe we can get close enough to walk from the docks?"

"It's further inland. We're going to need a car."

"I think I can help with that," Nina said, and both men watched her as she pulled out her phone, pushed a couple buttons and turned the screen toward them.

The map of the surrounding area popped up, and a cartoon car started moving slowly, turning onto Bayshore Lane and heading in their general direction.

"What the hell?" Jaime said.

"It's grenade proof." Nina shrugged. "The mechanic was telling me all about how it could withstand almost any explosion."

"I didn't know you could call it with your phone," Alex said. "That's fantastic."

"I thought it was silly, but now, I'm kind of glad."

"We need to get to shore and hide. We need to make sure it's not being followed."

Jaime stood, taking the helm from Nina and steering the yacht while Nina went to sit with Alex, still watching the car move along the map.

Alex leaned against her, hugging her close and kissing her cheek.

"Good thing you had your phone," he said.

She turned her head until her lips were against his ear, watching Jaime out the side of her eye to make sure he wasn't listening.

"That's not all I have in my pocket," she whispered. "Everything is going to be alright."

They huddled together as Jaime guided the yacht to the shore, cutting the engine and setting the GPS anchor since there was nowhere to dock. They took the inflatable dingy to shore, leaving the yacht where it was and finding a place to hide close by.

Nina selected an address a block away, locking the position where the car was supposed to They watched from down the block, waiting for the car to appear, then watching for a while longer before they finally approached the car. Jaime covered the door as Alex opened it, but the car was empty.

Jaime went to get into the driver's seat, but Nina stopped him, jumping in and using her thumb on the scanner to start the engine.

"This was money well-spent," Alex said, getting into the passenger seat still favoring his arm. "And not a scratch on it."

Jaime called out the address and Nina typed it into the navigation system, then pulled away from the curb and calmly drove through the streets while Jaime watched out the windows, his paranoia evident. When they arrived at their destination, Nina was surprised by all the cars in the well-lit parking lot.

"The DEA operates at odd hours," Jaime explained. "I'm sorry to have to do this, but Alex, I'm going to have to cuff you."

Alex held out his hands and Jaime pulled a pair of zip ties out of a zipper on the inside of his jacket. Nina killed the engine, parking near the building and getting out before Jaime could cuff her, too. Jaime shook his head, apparently amused.

"I wasn't going to cuff you."

"That's good," Nina said. "I've had to stop myself from whooping your ass twice tonight. If there's a third time, you might not be so lucky."

Chapter 15

They were ushered into an interview room, but almost immediately, they attempted to separate Alex and Nina.

"She's not involved in this," Alex said. "We haven't known each other long."

The agent running the interview arched a brow at Nina's slightly swollen belly, giving Jaime a look that spoke volumes. Nina wanted to melt into the floor, but she stood her ground. She wasn't going to let them belittle her.

"I'm not a tart, ," she said, glaring at the man. "Do you want to take down a cartel, or do you want to discuss how Alex Conrad is a better man than you in every way that counts?"

The man had the good sense to look embarrassed, turning to a new tactic.

"We need something to take to a judge if you want immunity. Your house is gone, and everything inside is destroyed. We might be able to salvage something, but there's no guarantee."

"I've worked for *Cienfuegos* for most of my life. I'm sure I have something you can use."

The agent slid a notepad to Alex.

"Write down names. Every name you can think of, where they're located, what they do and where they are in the hierarchy."

"Not without a deal. I'm not going to give you everything I have and watch you go back on every promise that you make. If I go to jail, I'm dead."

"You took that chance when you decided to run drugs."

"He never decided to do anything," Nina shot back, too angry to contain herself. "He was a kid. He's one of the good guys."

"Lady, where I'm from, the good guys don't launder money for the bad guys."

Nina sat back, her anger rising. She didn't know what she expected, but it sure wasn't this. They were acting like what Alex had wouldn't buy him a sandwich, let alone keep him out of jail.

She leaned back, her phone pressing against her hip. She shifted uncomfortably, then took her phone out and furrowed her brow at the notification symbol on the lock screen that she didn't recognize.

She looked up, but the agents were ignoring her, still trying to convince Alex to turn over names without any written agreements. Keeping her phone under the table, she used her fingerprint to open the screen and clicked on the icon. The prompt asked her if she would like to download emergency files to this device or sign in later. The header above said

Emergency Flare, but Nina wasn't sure what that was. Then, it hit her.

When she'd set up the software, she'd clicked the option to send what was on her laptop to her phone through the cloud. Everything that had been on her laptop, including the real time updates from the locations she'd updated that day, was in the cloud, waiting for her to access it. She clicked the option to sign in later, then looked up at the men and smiled.

"I have something y'all will want," she said, letting the southern slang out before she could stop herself. "But if you want it, you're going to have to have a judge sign off on a written deal. If he spends a day in jail, the deal is off."

"You couldn't possibly have anything that good," the agent said, but Jaime had already perked up.

Alex looked at her, but she was afraid to get her hopes up. *Would it be enough to keep him out of jail?*

"Fine, what do you have?" the agent asked, his voice gruff.

"I have access to the financial accounts proving that *Cienfuegos* was laundering money through these properties."

"Your laptop was destroyed in the explosion," Jaime scoffed.

"It was, but you're a fool if you think that's the only access I had."

"We'll seize your phone and access it."

"You can't. It's not on my phone, and it's not written down anywhere. I have the proof, and I can produce hardcopies of the proof, but without this," she tapped her head, "you're not getting into the files."

"Give us a minute," the man said, motioning with his head to Jaime to go out into the hall.

When they left, Nina leaned close, whispering softly in his ear.

"That's not the only computer I backed up."

"I want to ask how, but maybe I don't want to know."

"You're probably right."

"Hold onto that, we may need it later."

She nodded, rolling her chair back to where it had been before the men returned.

Jaime sat down across from her.

"What do you want?"

"Protection, and no jail time in exchange for testimony. And I don't mean some safehouse for months while we wait for trial, then shipping us off to some other state when it's all over. I mean real protection, and new identities so we can start fresh." She looked to Alex. "Anything else?"

"You have about covered it."

"We can't put you into WitSec until after court, so you'll have to stay in a safehouse for a few weeks."

"Weeks? Can you be sure of that?" Alex asked.

"Maybe less if we can get the judge to fast track the case. I've been gathering evidence for years, and whatever you have is in one place. Since the case is going to hinge on the financial proof and testimony, we should have it before the judge quickly. This is a big deal."

"What about at the court; how will you protect us there?"

"You probably won't testify," Jaime told her. "As cases go, your verbal testimony is almost useless. It's the hardcopies that will win the case. As for Alex, we'll do what we can, but nothing is one hundred percent, especially when the cartels are involved."

"That's as good as we can give you," the other agent confirmed.

"Can we have a moment to talk about it?"

"Sure."

They left, and Nina turned to Alex, searching his face for comfort.

"We're going to be okay," he said. "With your proof and the insurance, we're valuable to them."

She knew that "insurance" was the flash drive in her pocket, which she wasn't going to give up unless she had to.

"What about court?"

"They have no control over that. Even with metal detectors and every other precaution, there's still a chance that one of Carlos's men can get through."

"I don't want to risk it."

"In jail, I'll be dead within the hour. This is the better deal."

"I'm not giving them anything until I have something official."

"I agree."

"That would be best."

"Alex, I'm scared."

He smiled, leaning over so their foreheads were touching, his hands still cuffed together.

"You jumped off a balcony, drove a highspeed yacht away from danger, and found a way to get us here safely, all while managing to save the evidence we need to make sure we walk away from this free to start a new life together. There's nothing they can say or do that you can't handle. Don't let anyone tell you you're anything less than a bad ass."

"Thank you."

"Thank *you*. You probably saved my life."

Jaime and the other agent came in then, and Nina nodded.

"When you have something in writing, we'll talk."

"We've already called the judge. An agent is headed there now to get his signature, then we'll take you to the safehouse." Jaime turned his attention to Alex. "If you run, or try to get away, all deals are off."

Alex nodded, then held out his hands so Jaime could cut the plastic cuffs. The moment the cuff fell away, he had his arm around Nina, holding her tight. She melted into him, the weight of the last few hours heavy on her heart. Everything was going to be okay, but before that, it was going to be some of the hardest months of her life. She didn't know if she was ready for it, but with Alex by her side, she was willing to give it a try.

Jaime was looking at her, but she couldn't figure out why. When he finally spoke, his words shocked her.

"You were amazing tonight," he said. "You fooled me in the office. I totally bought your little show."

Alex looked at her, an amused smirk on his face, but she just shrugged.

"And I know you and Alex were on the second story when the first grenade went off. I know stronger women that would have crumbled under so much pressure, but you did what needed to be done and managed to stay calm. I know we've had our differences, but I was really impressed."

"Thank you. I think that's the nicest thing you've ever said to me."

"I'm sure you're right. Undercover work is hard, and after working on this for five years, you shook things up. I was worried you were going to ruin everything."

"I sorta did. Alex announced he was leaving *Cienfuegos* because of me, and that's why the house is demolished."

"If she hadn't come into my life and made me see what I was risking, things would have stayed the same. She's the reason I walked away, and that made Carlos mad. His men were sloppy."

"If they had waited a few hours, most of us would have been asleep," Jaime agreed. "They could have taken out the guards one at a time, then surprised you in bed."

Nina felt ill at the thought. Jaime was right; they had survived because Carlos had taken Alex's betrayal personally and reacted before he had a chance to think. His men didn't have time to prepare, and because of that, the attack had been a complete disaster by Carlos's standards.

She never thought she'd see the day when her survival was someone else's failure.

She laid her head on Alex's shoulder, trying to hold herself together in front of the agents. Having Jaime there was surreal, his badge clipped to his shirt as if he hadn't just spent the better part of five years deep undercover with a drug cartel. But this was the real him, not the part he'd played to get what he needed from Alex.

She had to drag her thoughts away from all the people who'd died at Alex's mansion today. For the most part, she'd been welcomed with open arms by Alex's staff and now, most of those people were gone. If any survived. The only one she knew for sure had survived was Jaime, and he'd been an ass to her from day one.

Suddenly, his behavior made sense, at least in Nina's mind.

"Were you trying to run me off?" she asked without preamble, picking her head up so she could meet Jaime's gaze.

His expression said it all, but she wanted to hear it from him, so she pressed.

"Were you an ass to me because you were trying to run me off?"

Jaime looked like he was trying to come up with something to say, but in the end, he went with honesty.

"Yes."

"Why?"

"It was obvious that you didn't know who he was; *what* he was. You're fresh out of college with your entire life ahead of you. I didn't want that to be ruined."

"And you couldn't just tell me and risk your cover."

"Exactly. It's complicated, but that about sums it up."

"I thought you were jealous."

She laughed at herself, thinking back to every encounter they'd had now that she knew who Jaime was. She felt a little foolish, but that only meant that he was good at his job. It had taken her until he revealed that he was DEA to realize that he wasn't just some thug trying to stay close to the boss. He was that good.

"I was worried about how your presence would interfere with my access to Alex. He spent a lot of time with you, and I got shut out of things that I wouldn't have before. When he went to that meeting with Carlos and he went without me, I was sure that he'd decided to groom you to be his second in command instead of me. I was angry about that.

That's why I was rough with you in Alex's office, and I'm sorry."

Nina fought the smirk that nearly spread across her face. *It looks like Jaime isn't the only good actor in this room*, she thought. He probably didn't even know she'd been in Alex's computer, but she wasn't going to tip her hand now. If Jaime knew that, then he might realize she had more information than she was willing to give up right now. It was better if he kept thinking she was just a pretty face.

This time, she did smile.

"I'm afraid to ask," Jaime said, the gruffness that had been his thug persona's trademark completely gone.

"It's nothing," she said. "I just never thought I'd see the day where Jaime Peña cared enough about me to try to run me off."

"It's Agent Garcia," he said. "Miguel Garcia."

"That's going to take some getting used to," Alex muttered.

Nina felt bad for Alex. He'd trusted Jaime with everything, and now he was finding out that Jaime wasn't the person he'd thought he was. She could tell Alex was upset that he'd trusted a DEA agent more than the rest of his crew.

"It's kind of like finding out the nice, rich man who made you feel like a princess is really working for a drug cartel," Nina said, elbowing Alex playfully and ignoring the agents.

Alex laughed.

"I guess you're right," he said, still chuckling. "I never thought of it that way."

She was about to say something more when there was a knock on the door and an agent burst in, rushing to where Jaime and the other agent were sitting with an official looking piece of paper in his hand.

The two agents read it over, then handed it to Alex and Nina to read. Nina read it over his shoulder as the weight of everything slowly pressed down on her.

"I won't be able contact Jasmine ever again?" she asked, shocked by this more than anything laid out in the order.

"You can't contact anyone from your past. Once you're in WitSec, Nina Wilson will cease to exist," Jaime said. "The alternative is leaving yourself open to retaliation. Even though we're going to arrest dozens of these criminals thanks to you, we won't get them all. You'll have a bounty on your head for the rest of your life. Contacting old friends is the quickest way to open the door and leave yourself vulnerable."

"Think of your baby," the other agent said.

"I don't need you to tell me to think of *my* child," she shot back. "That's all I've been doing since I found out."

The agent held his hands up as if to surrender, and Nina sat back, trying to calm herself.

"I can't believe the nerve," she muttered, glaring daggers at the agent, then turning her attention back to the state's offer.

When they'd finally read through the entire thing, Alex looked up at Nina.

"Are you okay with everything in here?"

"As long as we're together, I'm fine with it," she said. "I don't want to die."

"I won't let that happen," he said, pointing to the bandaged wound on his shoulder. "I took a bullet for you. That has to mean something."

"I know that's right," she said, smiling. "I still can't believe you got shot."

He shrugged, then winced.

"It could have been much worse. I could have lost you."

The agent sighed, but Jaime was grinning from ear to ear. *Miguel*, she corrected herself. She had to start thinking about him being Miguel and not Jaime. It was going to take some doing.

"If you're done with the sappy stuff, we need to get this signed so we can get moving. There's a short window of time, and without the information you have, arresting anyone tonight might be pointless. I don't want to have to cut them loose tomorrow because the DA says we don't have enough evidence."

"I'll need a laptop," she said. "And internet access."

Miguel took one out of a bag sitting on the floor beside him, logging on and sliding it across the table after Alex and Nina had both signed the order and kept a copy for themselves. Nina logged onto the virtual storage, downloading every file she had, but leaving a copy in the cloud for her own form of insurance. Miguel had no idea that she still had access to the originals, but that wasn't her problem.

He wasn't the only one who was good at keeping secrets.

Chapter 16

Before the ink even had a chance to dry, they were whisked away, taken to an unmarked car and loaded into the back seat. Only Miguel got in the car, leaving the other agents to plan the takedown while Miguel got Alex and Nina secured. Nina took one last look at her Audi A8L as they drove away, then focused on the road ahead.

Alex saw her, taking her hand and squeezing.

"I'll get you another car," he said.

"I know they'll be other cars, I just really loved that one. I know you loved your house, so I guess I shouldn't complain."

"A house can be replaced, and so can a car. You are the only thing I care about."

Nina caught Miguel looking at her in the rearview mirror, his eyes the same hard ones she'd come to know from her time with "Jaime."

"How long before you go back to being normal?" Nina asked him.

"What do you mean?"

"I think you know. I can see it in your eyes. One minute, you're Miguel, then you slip back into 'Jaime'. I guess after five years being a thug comes naturally."

He stiffened.

"I never forgot who I was," he said almost angrily. "The law is what's most important. My friendship with Alex was just a means to an end."

"I don't believe that," Nina challenged. "And I don't think you do, either. It's just us. You can be honest."

But Miguel stood his ground.

"It was just a job."

"Why aren't you taking down Carlos with the rest of the agents?" Nina asked, already in too deep to worry about pissing Miguel off.

She had questions, and she didn't know when she'd have another chance to ask him.

"I have information that no one else has, and I have to testify. If I get killed before the trial, the state's case weakens. Your evidence is great, but they need what I have, too."

"So, you're going to be stuck in the safehouse as well?" Alex said.

"Unfortunately, yes. But I'll have my own location. They don't keep criminals with the agents."

He smirked when he delivered that last dig, and Nina glared at him.

"You remember what I said about not getting lucky a third time," she warned. "Don't push me."

"Well, this is where you get out," he said, pulling into the parking lot of a McDonald's and parking beside another dark colored car. "I'll see you in court."

He unlocked the child locks on the driver's side rear door and leaving the other lock engaged so they both had to exit on Nina's side of the car. The other car had backed in so that opening the doors created a chute, protecting them from gunfire and herding them into the other car without a hitch.

"Why do I feel like a wild animal?" Nina muttered, then addressed the men in the front seat. "Hit the drive-thru, I'm starving."

"We'll order food at the safehouse," one of the two agents in the front seat said, but Nina was already shaking her head.

"You don't want to see me when I'm hungry," she shot back, and Alex rushed to cover his mouth to contain his laughter.

She glared at the men, then finally, they gave in.

"Not a peep out of either of you," the agent driving warned. "And no eating in my car."

Nina raised an eyebrow and shook her head.

"Don't even start with me. I'm tired, I'm pregnant and I'm hungry.. This is not a fight you want to get into."

The agents looked at each other, then the driver shrugged.

"Whatever," he grumbled. "Just don't make a mess."

By the time they hit the highway, Nina was almost done and feeling so much better.

"Your kid is hungry all the time," she joked, snuggling against Alex in the back seat as the car headed north. "I can't wait until December."

"You know the trial might last longer than that," one of the agents said.

"Not if you do your job, it won't," she countered, but she knew he was right, even if she didn't want to admit it. "I'm not having this baby in a safehouse."

"She's feisty. You might be better off taking your chances with the cartel, Alex."

She ignored the agent, too tired to deal with them anymore. She just wanted to get to the safehouse and get in bed. She would worry about the fact that she didn't have a thing except the clothes on her back and her phone. Everything else was destroyed with the house, and that was more than she could handle right now.

Tomorrow, they would worry about getting clothes and comfort items to pass the time until court was over. Right now, the only thing on her mind was crawling into bed with Alex and forgetting all about what had happened that night.

She was starting to doze off when the car slowed, then backed into a garage. Alex was still awake, watching her sleep and tenderly stroking his thumb across her hand. She smiled sleepily at him, and when the agents called the all clear, she let him lead her inside.

The house was small, with three rooms; a bedroom,kitchen dining room combination, and a living room. All the windows were covered with blackout curtains, and multiple screens in the kitchen showed cameras from every angle, covering the yard and the streets beyond on all four sides.

It was like a fortress, but even though she knew they were safe, she wasn't sure she'd ever *feel* as safe as she had in Alex's house.

"Damnit, I miss Jaime," Nina muttered.

"I do, too," Alex admitted.

"You'll take this room. Someone will bring your things once they've been checked."

"We don't have things," Alex said. "It all went up with the house."

"In that case, write your sizes down and we'll send someone for clothes and anything else you need. Plan on being here at least six months, though we're trying to push it through the courts. These guys make bail and flee to Cuba. We're going to keep that from happening if we can."

The man handed a pocket-sized spiral notepad to Nina. She quickly jotted down what she needed, then handed the pad off to Alex. When Alex handed it to the agent, he looked at her list and sighed.

"I'm assuming that none of this is negotiable."

"Smart man," she said.

She turned, walking through the bedroom door without waiting to see if Alex followed her. She was exhausted, and even though the bed was nowhere near as nice as the one she'd been sleeping on for weeks, she was asleep before her head hit the pillow.

She had no idea when Alex joined her, but she woke up once in the night with his arms wrapped tightly around her. She snuggled against him, kissing him while he slept, then closing her eyes and letting herself drift off.

A thin ray of bright sunshine had found its way through a slit on the edge of the heavy curtains when she awoke to a knock at their door.

She groaned, getting up and answering the door. She almost panicked when she didn't recognize the face behind the door, but the man quickly identified himself.

"Agent Rivers with the DEA," he said, showing his badge. "I thought you might want to have some lunch and make sure these clothes fit."

He was young, his eyes still bright with ambition and passion for the job. She knew it was only a matter of time before he'd seen too much, and that changed. But for now, he was exuberant, and that was already rubbing off on Nina even though she was still so exhausted.

"Lunch?" she queried, not sure she'd heard him right.

"You slept through breakfast. It's probably a reaction to all that adrenaline. Did you know that when the body is stressed by some kind of catastrophic event, it floods your system with adrenaline, which is why you can do things you never could before? Like jumping from a building without getting hurt and dodging bullets. It's actually very interesting, and—"

"Slow down there, Einstein. It's too early for this much talking."

"It's actually quarter past noon."

She gave him a withering look.

"Right," he said, nodding. "Well, anyway, your clothes are in the living room, and here's the menu. I'll put in the order as soon as you're ready."

"Thanks," she said, closing the door slowly so she didn't slam it in his face, but made it clear she was done talking for now.

"He's peppy," Alex said, still in the bed.

"That's way too much energy for me." She laughed. "They want us to order lunch."

She sat beside him on the bed and he kissed her cheek.

"How are you feeling today?"

"Tired. Raw. A little numb."

"That will pass."

"I'm glad." She circled the items she wanted with the pencil Agent Rivers had given her, then passed it off to Alex.

"Let's get dressed. It's time to face the day."

There were bags of clothes in the living room as promised, along with everything else they'd requested. Nina was helping Alex gather up their things when the show on the television disappeared and a *Breaking News Alert* ticker filled the screen.

"We interrupt this program to bring you breaking news," a steady, almost bland female voice announced. "The DEA has mounted a mass sting today, bringing in nearly one hundred members of the *Cienfuegos* drug cartel, including cartel leader, Carlos Managua. This is part of a five-year investigation into the cartel's activity in Miami and surrounding areas, and their ties to the city of the same name in Cuba. We'll have more as this story progresses, so keep your televisions tuned in."

"One hundred?" Nina asked, incredulous.

"It was a big operation," Agent Rivers offered. "Most of those men will do minimal time. They're not after the foot soldiers, they're after Carlos and his closest confidants. It's good you got out when you did, Mister Conrad. Very lucky."

"When do we testify?" Nina asked.

"There will be hearings to determine bail, if any, then more hearings while the lawyers attempt to stall. You'll give your taped deposition in the room in the back, and when they're ready for Alex to testify, they will let us know. You probably won't be called, but it is a possibility."

"I can do that," she said.

"I'm sure you can. From what I've seen, you were the catalyst in all this. Anyone who can bring down a major player in a cartel and convince him to turn state's evidence can probably do anything she sets her mind to."

"I like this one," she said to Alex. "Let's make sure that he's always our guard."

"As the low man on the totem pole, I'll likely be your main agent, so you'll probably get your wish there."

"At least something is going my way," she said, picking up the bags and leaving the agents to their television.

She put the bags on the bed, rummaging through the clothes until she found an outfit that spoke to her, then she gathered the clothes and toiletries up and headed to the bathroom. When Alex followed her in, she didn't argue. She was hoping he would.

Together, they washed away the events of the past twenty-four hours until Nina finally felt like herself again.

When Alex moved up against her, his meaning was clear. This shower was a tighter fit, and somehow, that brought its own level of excitement though it didn't compare to the places they'd made love before.

Nina arched against him, warm water spilling over their bodies as he rode her hard and fast. They climaxed together a few minutes later, Alex holding her hips as he pounded into her from behind. She sighed when he slipped out of her, turning to face him and wrapping her arms around his neck and kissing him passionately. Her tongue slipped between his lips as she deepened the kiss, then pulled back and smiled.

"That was exactly what I needed," she said, heart still racing.

"Me too." He playfully brushed his thumb over her nipple, causing her body to twitch.

She giggled, then turned serious, totally oblivious to the water that was starting to turn cool.

"We're going to make it through this," Alex assured her before she could voice her fears. "I know it doesn't feel like it, but we will make it out."

"I believe you. I'm just so scared. Not for myself. Even if I have to testify, it's probably only going to be one day, maybe two. But you have over a decade with *Cienfuegos*, and every time you walk into that courtroom, your life is in danger."

"I'm going to be fine," he told her.

"I hope you're right."

He reached behind her and turned the water off, stepping out of the shower first, then helping her out. He took his time toweling her off, then got dressed while she did the same. By the time they were dressed and ready to leave the room, lunch was served.

They sat down at the table with the two agents, and Nina couldn't help but think back to the day before, sharing breakfast with everyone like one big family. It didn't matter that they were thugs, they were human. If she'd had dinner with them the night before, she probably would have died with them.

A single tear slid down her cheek before she managed to stop herself. Alex took her hand and squeezed, and her heart nearly burst with the sadness hanging between them.

"I'm going to miss them, too," Alex said softly.

And with that, the flood gates opened, and Nina turned her head, burying her face in Alex's shoulder as he held her there in front of the agents, and let her cry until she ran out of tears for people she knew that the world would never miss.

Chapter17

Five Months Later

It was late November when Nina was finally called to the stand, something she'd been simultaneously dreading and wishing she could get over with for more than five months. Nina sat in court, trying her best to stay calm as the Carlos's lawyer attempted to tear her apart on the stand. Nina had been practicing for months, and she let him waste his breath trying to scare her. She'd been through more in the past year than this pompous, bloated, egotistical ass-hat had been in his entire life.

"Now, when you first noticed the discrepancy in the numbers, why didn't you immediately call the authorities? Why did you wait until you were in the custody of agents to share this information?"

"It all happened in the same day. I didn't have time to report it to anyone."

"You had time to tell Mister Conrad, did you not?"

"I did."

"Why would you tell the very man who was at the center of these illegal activities that you knew what he was doing? Didn't you fear for your safety?"

"No."

"Are you aware that Alex Conrad has a reputation for being ruthless; that people have died after crossing him?"

"Objection!" one of the state's attorneys called out. "That's heresay."

"Sustained," the judge said. "Mister Bartlett, you will keep your questions based on facts, not urban legends and heresay."

"My apologies, Judge. Withdrawn," Mister Bartlett said, but it was the same thing he'd said several times already.

It seemed that the sleazy lawyer's primary technique was to sneak outlandish claims into the testimony, and then withdraw them. The end result was the same; the jury heard the claims, and Mister Bartlett hoped to color the jury against Alex and everyone else who stepped on the stand.

"Moving on. Is it true, Nina, that you are pregnant with Mister Conrad's child?"

"Yes, meaning you are pregnant, Nina?"

He was using her name to get under her skin, calling everyone else by their surname except for her in hopes of degrading her and throwing her off balance. But she'd been warned against this game of his, too, and she was ready.

"Looks like we both are, Patrick."

The courtroom erupted with laughter, and the judge began banging her gavel, calling for order, but a quick glance told Nina that the judge was struggling to hide her amusement and stay impartial. It looked like Nina wasn't the only one who despised Patrick Bartlett and his three-ring circus act. He was making a mockery of the legal system, and Nina was left wondering how he stayed in business.

But she knew that arrogance won cases, and Patrick Bartlett had arrogance on lock. No one would ever accuse the bloated moron of being humble.

It was clear that she had knocked him off balance, and he was struggling to find something that would give him back the control he thought he had.

He was pacing, setting the stage as if he were the ringmaster and not a lawyer in a federal court. In any other situation, Nina would have walked away, but she was stuck on the stand, raised up for everyone to see and scrutinize, her every word weighed for honesty.

She couldn't wait to get this over with, but there would be a redirection from the prosecution when the defense was through with her, and then the jury would deliberate and they would finally be done with all this. It had been a long, nearly six months, and she couldn't wait to walk away and never look back.

"You're funny," Mister Bartlett finally said, advancing on the witness stand pretty quickly. "I wonder what your family thinks of all this?"

"My parents are gone."

"I'm sorry to hear that, truly," he said, placing his hand over his heart, but she knew that he already knew about them.

What is he doing? Nina wondered. She didn't bother thanking him for his feigned condolences.

"It must be hard, having no one in this situation. It's no wonder you picked up everything to move here to be with Mister Conrad. I wonder if that was your plan all along; to trap the billionaire with a pregnancy. Is that why you and your friend just *happened* to show up in Conrad's club that night? Did you and your friend—Jasmine Parks, is it—did you plan all this out, not realizing what kind of monster Alex Conrad really was?"

Nina's mouth dropped open at the mention of Jazzy's name. In a panic, she looked to the prosecuting attorneys for guidance, anything, but they were already approaching the bench. The judge motioned to Patrick Bartlett, her face angry.

"Are you insane?" the state's attorney hissed when Patrick was within earshot. "What are you doing, revealing the name of family friends."

"She's not family," he said smugly, then turned his head ever so slightly so that he was giving Nina the side eye. "She's not listed as one of the protected identities and it speaks to Nina's credibility. It's important that the jury knows her motivation for getting involved with a drug lord in the first place."

He was still trying to get under her skin, and he was so close that Nina was tempted to jump out of the witness stand and tear him up right there in front of everyone, but that would only get her thrown in jail. She would have to wait until court was over for the day to call Jazzy and warn her, if it wasn't already too late. She was still stuck on the stand until this mess was over.

Thank God this is the last day, she thought, taking a deep breath and placing her hand on her stomach when she felt a tiny foot pressing against the inside of her. She wasn't going to let this man get to her.

"You're done, Mister Bartlett," the judge said. "Prosecutor, your witness."

Nina let out a sigh of relief when the sweet, petite blonde walked up to the stand and began her redirection, guiding Nina through telling her story, then thanking her for her bravery before turning over the floor.

Nina took her time getting down from the stand, her heavily pregnant belly making her look like she was waddling.

She sat down in the seat behind Alex, not allowed to sit with him during the trial. He gave her the thumbs-up sign under the table and she smiled. She'd done her best, but the little weasel had managed to get to her more than once. Hopefully, the district attorney would be just as happy with her performance on the stand, and everything Alex had shared over the past few months. Their lives depended on it, and a big part of their protection depended on the jury coming back with a guilty verdict.

The DEA made it clear that they were avoiding jail by testifying, but if the jury came back without a guilty verdict, there was a chance that Alex and Nina would be on their own. But that didn't scare her as much as they seemed to think it would, and she was certain that they were bluffing, trying to ensure that Nina and Alex would give everything they had to save themselves. What they didn't know is that Nina had more than she'd given them, and what she had would keep them safe no matter what happened in court.

As expected, Patrick Bartlett's closing arguments were over the top and almost laughable, and by the looks of the faces in the jury box, Nina was almost positive that the jury wasn't buying it.

When he was done, the prosecution sent the same petite, passionate blonde that had done most of the questioning, and by the time she was done, she had the jury in her hands, and Nina knew that Carlos Managua was going to spend the rest of his life in prison, as would most of his men. This case would be used to put most if not all of the over one hundred men and women who had been arrested in the sweep away, and Nina and Alex would walk away from Miami and everything that had happened to them in the past six months.

It was all up to the jury, and there was nothing she could do about that now.

The lawyers finished, sitting down while the judge instructed the jury before they left to deliberate. Nina and Alex were ushered through a side door as they had been every day Nina had attended court, taking them to the waiting car at the back of the courthouse before anyone else was dismissed from court.

Nina went out first, agents leading her to the car as they always had, everyone on edge when they exited the court. She'd been warned that this was the most dangerous time for them, and she was already on edge, watching every shadow cast by the massive stone building as they rushed to the car waiting in the back.

She saw the man out of the corner of her eye, but before she could say anything, she heard the *pop! pop! pop!* and someone nearby screamed. She tried to turn, to see if Alex was okay, but strong hands suddenly had her by the arms as two agents all but carried her to the car at a dead run.

"Alex!" she shouted. "Where's Alex!"

"Run!" a man said, pulling her faster.

She managed to turn in time to catch the man with the gun being tackled by DEA agents, but she didn't see Alex anywhere.

The agent at the car opened the back door of the SUV, and Nina turned, yanking free of the two agents, and searching the crowd for Alex.

Her heart dropped when she saw him, limp and covered in blood, being half-dragged, half-carried by a pair of agents who were covered in his blood.

"Alex!" she screamed, trying to run toward him, but the agents got ahold of her again.

They held her back while she fought, yelling Alex's name over and over. A crowd appeared from around the building, running as if in a herd. It took Nina a second to realize that it was the media, running toward the sound of gunfire when everyone else was running away.

She tried to pull away from the agents, but they were stronger than her, and they weren't going to be surprised into letting her go again. Fingers dug painfully into her flesh. Pulling her off her feet, they shoved her into the back seat and Agent Rivers slid in beside her, blocking her from getting out the open door.

They loaded Alex into another car, with reporters right behind them, clamoring to get the best shot for the news. The second SUV peeled out, heading toward the nearest hospital.

Nina cried out in rage and despair, hitting Agent Rivers in the chest and screaming at him.

"You said he would be alright," she said, pummeling him in the chest over and over while he grunted and attempted to get his arms around her.

When he finally pinned her against him, she broke down in tears, huge, gut-wrenching sobs wracking through her body. It didn't matter what the jury came back with now, she didn't care. She'd lost the only man she'd ever loved, and now the only person she had left in the world was doing somersaults in her belly, no idea that the world they were coming into was a cruel, cruel place. They would have each other, and no one else.

Suddenly, she remembered what had happened in court and she pulled away from Agent Rivers.

"Jazzy. You have to make sure she's okay. That asshole said her name right in front of Carlos's men. They'll find her, and I can't lose her, too."

"An agent has already picked her up. Now that her life has been compromised, she'll be offered similar protection."

"Don't let anything happen to Jazzy. She's all I got left."

"I'm sorry about this," Agent Rivers said. "We're going to a safehouse to debrief, and as soon as the verdict comes back, you'll be taken to your new home."

Nina nodded her understanding, but she felt numb. How could this happen at the last second?

They'd done everything they had been asked and all the agents had to do was protect them. It was that easy. Wasn't it?

She leaned back against the seat and closed her eyes, letting the tears spill over her cheeks unchecked. When Rivers took her hand she yanked it away, and he didn't try to stop her.

Without opening her eyes, she said the only thing she could think of in that moment.

"You promised me he would be okay."

"I'm so sorry. I didn't want you to have to go through this."

"*You promised,*" she whispered.

The Final Chapter

Nina sat on the sofa in the safehouse, watching the news cycle through the same stories over and over. They were doing a recap of the trial and the DEA sweep leading up to it, building anticipation for the verdict as Miami held its breath, waiting for the verdict.

Nina felt raw and completely numb, completely detached from what was happening on the screen. Her dinner sat untouched on the table, and she had no idea when Agent Rivers had placed a soft blanket around her shoulders, wrapping her in warmth that was stifling and comforting all at once. She'd been sitting there for hours, unmoving, completely oblivious to everything going on around her.

There was a knock on the door, but Nina didn't move. She didn't care who was there.

An agent walked in first, then he was shoved aside so hard that he almost fell over, and Jazzy burst in, rushing to Nina.

"Girl, what did you get yourself into?" Jasmine said, sitting on the couch beside her and hugging her tight.

"Oh Jazzy," Nina sobbed. "I'm so sorry about all this."

"Shh," Jasmine said. "It's alright. Everything is gonna be alright."

Nina held her friend tight, too tired to cry anymore. She looked up at the agents, still angry with everything that had happened, but thankful that they had gotten to Jasmine in time.

There was more movement in the doorway, and when the familiar face appeared in the doorway, Nina felt faint.

She pulled herself out of Jasmine's arms, standing up and walking to the door in a daze. He stood there, his shirt stained with an impossible amount of dry blood, a sad, crooked smile on his face.

"I thought you were dead," she said.

He caught her hand before it connected with his face, kissing her open palm before pulling her into his arms. This time, she cried tears of relief and joy so powerful that she struggled to stay standing.

Alex was alive. She didn't know how or why, but he was alive.

She pulled out of his grasp, glaring at him, but he held his ground.

"How could you do that to me?"

"We needed your reaction to be realistic," Agent Rivers said. "In order to have a fresh start, Carlos Managua and his men must believe that Alex is dead. They would only come after you to hurt him. But it's hard to fake that kind of reaction, and we needed you to do exactly what you did."

"Is that why you said you were sorry about all this instead of sorry about Alex?"

"It was. I felt bad putting you through that, but it was for the greater good."

"The greater good can kiss my ass."

Alex unbuttoned his shirt and removed his vest, handing it to one of the agents. He winced when Nina touched the fist-sized bruise on his ribs.

"That one hurt like hell," he said.

"Good."

"I didn't expect sympathy," he said, chuckling. "I'm really sorry. I hope you can forgive me."

"Of course, I forgive you. Doesn't mean you're out of the doghouse, though."

"Sounds good to me," he said, laughing.

"Why did you have to get shot like that? Isn't there an easier way to make them think you're dead?"

"Yes, there is, but someone already blew up my house, so we had to go with plan B."

The television announced an update, and they turned as one when the anchor announced that the jury was back with a verdict after only seven hours of deliberation.

"Here we go," Agent Rivers said as they gathered around the television.

The jury foreman stood, taking a deep breath before reading from the paper, his voice shaking, the paper trembling slightly in his hand.

"We, the jury, find the defendant, Carlos Efrain Managua, guilty on all charges."

The agents yelled in delight as one, startling the baby inside Nina as she stared, open-mouthed at the screen.

"That's it?" she said. "It's over?"

"It's over," Agent Rivers said. "You don't have to hear the name Carlos Managua ever again."

The camera panned around the courtroom, editing the footage to show the reaction of each section as the verdict was read over and over again in the background. Carlos Managua looked stunned by the verdict, but no reaction was as satisfying as that of his sleazebag lawyer. Patrick Bartlett's mouth dropped open in shock, and he turned to Carlos, fear in his eyes. Before anyone could react, Carlos swung hard, catching the lawyer square in the jaw with one giant fist. The lawyer staggered backward a few steps then fell to the ground.

"Serves his ass right," Nina said.

"Is that the man?" Jasmine asked.

"He is. He's the reason you're here with us."

"I guess I should thank him, but that worked, too."

"I'm sorry you were ripped away from your life because of me."

"Are you kidding? I was still looking for a job, and I was about to get kicked out of my apartment. I guess I need you to keep me on track."

"I guess." Nina laughed, hugging her friend.

"I hate to cut this short, but we need to move while people are still focused on the news. We can't risk anyone recognizing you or Alex."

"Where are we going?" Nina asked.

"I don't know," Agent Rivers said. "Suffice it to say that it's somewhere wonderful, and you won't be disappointed. That's all I know."

"I'll just gather our stuff, and—"

"No stuff," Agent Rivers said.

"Whatever," Nina said. "I won't miss a thing about this place."

The agents gave each of them a bulletproof vest and a jacket that read "DEA," and matching hats, then led the way out of the room.

The three of them positioned themselves randomly so that they didn't look like they were together, and anyone looking on would see a group of DEA agents and nothing more. Nina didn't bother looking around at the hotel as they walked through the courtyard. She didn't want to remember this place, and she wanted to leave this time behind.

They split up into three SUVs, the three of them ending up in the same back seat by design, a dark partition between them and the driver to block them from view of other motorists through the windshield. It was dark and wasn't likely to be a problem, but even the slightest chance of being seen was too much, and Nina was glad they took the extra precaution.

The radio was on in the back, the news reporting as it had on the TV.

"I'm really sick of this," Nina said, but Alex stopped her from turning the channel on their radio.

"Drug lord turned state's evidence, Alex Conrad was killed today as he left the courthouse, the subject in his slaying subdued immediately by agents," the man's voice said over the speaker. "His pregnant wife was taken away, presumably to a safehouse to wait out the results of the trial before being released."

"These people act like y'all are thugs," Jasmine said. "Shameful. At least your performance was convincing, Alex."

"I didn't have much of a choice. Rubber bullets hurt pretty bad and falling down was a natural reaction."

"I saw it on the TV," Jasmine continued. "I thought you were dead."

"Thanks."

"Where do you think they're taking us?" Jasmine asked.

"They wouldn't tell me. I think we're transferring from this car to another one at the halfway point, and maybe once more if they think we're being followed."

"That's comforting," Jasmine mumbled.

"It's necessary. We don't want to get into our new place and discover that they know where we are. I don't know about you, but I don't want to spend the rest of my life looking over my shoulder."

Nina was leaned back in the seat, watching the two of them banter back and forth, trying to ignore her discomfort. She was due in less than three weeks, and ever since Alex had been shot earlier in the day, she'd been having Braxton Hicks contractions. They were bearable but sitting in the car had her feeling really uncomfortable, and she couldn't wait to get out and walk around.

She pushed the pain to the back of her mind, focusing on the scenery out her window and trying to guess what their new house would be like. She knew they wouldn't be able to live in the luxury they had enjoyed before, but they could fill their house with what made them happy, and they would find a way to make it work. As long as she had Alex and Jasmine with her, everything was going to be alright.

They made the first switch as they had in the McDonald's parking lot so many months before, the cars nose to tail, back doors shielding them from view. The transfer was done so quickly that they were in the next SUV and leaving the back of the grocery store parking lot within ninety seconds.

Her contractions had calmed somewhat, and she chalked it up to the stress, finally letting herself relax enough to lean back and doze off while Jasmine and Alex passed the time talking about anything and everything that came up.

She was just starting to relax when the SUV slowed, and she looked out the window to see they were pulling up to their final transfer. Nina sat up, cringing when pain ripped through her.

"Are you alright?" Alex asked.

"I'm just cramping from sitting in one position for too long," she said, sliding across the seat toward the sedan that sat waiting for them.

When her feet hit the pavement, another shooting pain went through her abdomen, and she knew there was no explaining this one away. She grabbed Alex's arm to catch herself, moaning softly.

"Nina?" Alex asked.

"It's time, Alex."

"Time for what?" Jasmine said, then gasped. "Wait, now?"

"Now, what?" the confused agent who'd been driving the SUV asked.

But Alex was already pushing Nina into the new car, instructing Jasmine to get in the front seat.

"Drive!" he said, and the driver of the sedan stomped on the gas, tires spinning for an instant before they caught asphalt.

Nina breathed through the pain, leaning against Alex for support, her feet against the passenger door as the sedan whipped through traffic, finally screeching to a halt in front of the hospital maternity door. Nina reached into her pocket, putting the flash drive in Alex's hand. He took it and put it in his own pocket quickly, kissing the top of her head and holding her through another painful contraction.

A familiar voice shouted to be heard over her moans.

"No names. Let me handle everything."

Nina's head turned and she stared incredulous at the man in the driver's seat.

"Jaime?" she said, then remembered his name was Miguel.

"I said no names," he repeated, smiling. "I'll handle this, that's my job."

She nodded, and Jasmine opened the passenger door just in time for the nurse that came rushing forward.

"That was quick," Jasmine said.

"We know what it means when a car screeches to a halt like that." The nurse laughed, helping Nina into the wheelchair. "What's your name, mama?"

"TeLina," Miguel said. "I'll handle the paperwork while you get them to the room."

The nurse started to argue, but he produced his badge, and the nurse closed her mouth and nodded.

"Come on Mom and Dad, let's have a baby."

The nurse wheeled her through the halls, almost running Alex over more than once when she turned without warning. They stopped in a large room that looked more like a hotel room than a hospital room.

"Aren't you taking me to the delivery room?" she asked, trying to breathe as the pain increased.

"This is the delivery room. You're going to love it."

She disappeared, but another nurse took her place in an instant, getting Nina ready and in a hospital gown with practiced precision. A few moments later a doctor sailed into the room, way too peppy for Nina's taste and already scrubbed up and ready to go. The doctor took her place on a rolling chair, checking Nina and smiling at Alex.

"I hope you're ready now, because we're about to have a baby."

"I need medication," Nina said, but the doctor was already shaking her head.

"No time, honey. When I say now, I mean now. You've been in labor for hours."

Alex took her head in his hands, looking deep into her eyes and smiling.

"You've got this," he said, smiling. "You can do this. Just focus on me and breathe like we practiced, okay?"

"I can't do this," she said.

"Sure, you can," the peppy red-headed doctor said. "You've done the hard part, just keep breathing and push when you feel the urge."

Nina focused on Alex, copying his breathing and squeezing his fingers until she was sure she would break them with each push. When she felt a sudden relief and heard a baby's cry fill the room she fell back, tears of joy streaming down her face. The nurses rushed forward, wiping him down and setting him on Nina's chest.

When she looked down at the little head of curly hair, everything else melted away. Alex tenderly ran a single finger over the tiny little head, smiling at Nina when their eyes met.

"I told you, you could do it. Baby, he's beautiful."

"He?" she said. "I didn't even think to ask."

"Definitely a boy," the doctor said. "We'll clean up and be out of your way in a minute. Congratulations. You did good."

Nina thanked the doctor and smiled at Alex, then looked down at the tiny babe on her chest.

"I can't believe you're finally here," she whispered, tears still streaming down her face. "I love you so much."

"Does he have a name?" a nurse said from behind Alex.

"I had one in mind," she said. "But it's up to you."

"Gabriel Demarcus. After your dad and mine."

Alex nodded, too touched to speak.

"My stepfather would have loved you," he said finally. "My mother, too."

The nurse handed Alex the certificate and he wrote down the name, then handed the clipboard to Nina. She noticed that their names were already typed in the spaces provided, and she carefully signed her new name as it appeared on the birth certificate.

TeLina Jackson, wife of Vance Jackson.

Just like that, the nurse was gone and they were alone for a few minutes, just the three of them. Nina soaked in the peaceful feeling, head tilted and resting against Alex's.

"Does that flash drive have what I think it does on it?"

"Everything that was on your computer's desktop," she confirmed with a wry smile.

"You're perfect," he said.

"I know."

They were still laughing when Miguel and Jasmine breezed into the room, excitedly wishing them well and admiring Gabriel. Nina handed him off to Jasmine, who immediately took her phone out and took a selfie with the child.

Miguel scowled.

"I hope you have the GPS turned off on that phone."

"Relax," she said. "It doesn't have the SIM card in. I'm not an idiot."

"I never said you were," Miguel said, and Nina realized that he was looking at Jasmine much like the way Alex had looked at her in those early days.

He *liked* Jazzy. Things were about to get interesting, and it wasn't just because there was a new baby.

"Is this where we're living?" Nina asked Miguel, careful to keep her voice low.

"The house is close, outside the city limit of Jacksonville, so quiet and close-knit without being too far from the city."

"They said you should be able to go home tomorrow," Jasmine said. "We need to get some things for the house."

"We don't have anything for the baby," Nina fretted.

"I got ya, boo," Jasmine said, patting her hand.

"We'll be back in the morning," Miguel said.

"You're not staying here?" Nina asked.

"If you're not safe here, then you're not safe in this city," Miguel said. "Just remember your new names and don't offer too much information to the nurses. Get some rest. We'll be here first thing in the morning to pick you up."

They left Alex and Nina alone to be with their new addition. Nina couldn't stop staring at him, watching him breathe and move his lips in his sleep. She couldn't be sure because he was so little, but it looked like he had Alex's bright green eyes. He felt good against her skin, his hot little body warming hers in the cool room.

When the nurse brought a clear plastic bassinet into the room with Gabriel's name on a tag, she was loathed to put him in it.

"I'm not ready to let him out of my sight," she said to the nurse.

"He's not going anywhere," the nurse said, a hefty black woman with an obvious Louisiana accent. "The couch there pulls out for Dad, and you and Dad and baby jump right into being a family. If you need anything, push the button. When you can stand, make sure you walk around as much as you can. The bathroom has a shower and everything you need to make yourself at home."

"This is amazing. Do you have room service, too?"

She was only teasing, but the nurse smiled.

"We don't, but the cafeteria is open twenty-four hours in the maternity wing. I can take your little guy to the nursery and you and Dad can have something to eat."

When she saw Nina look worriedly in Gabriel's direction she patted her arm.

"Newborns sleep through most of their first day. He won't even notice you're gone. Take a shower and enjoy some peace and quiet. You don't know how many hot meals you're going to miss now that you have a baby."

Nina didn't need any more convincing than that.

*

They returned early in the morning as promised, and Jasmine handed Nina a freshly washed outfit with tiny blue whales all over it.

"This is cute, thank you."

"He's going to have to sleep in your room while the paint airs out for a couple days, but you're going to love his room."

"Paint?"

"Tiana was up all night putting the nursery together," Miguel said. "Your sister is quite handy."

Nina rolled her eyes.

"We don't even look like sisters," she whispered, but Miguel only laughed and shrugged.

Nina put the clothes on Gabriel, talking to him softly while she did. When the nurse appeared to check them out, Jasmine took Gabriel and put him in the car seat she'd brought to the hospital that morning, then tucked the blanket around him.

"Don't you look cute," Jasmine said. "Auntie's gonna spoil you rotten. Yes, she is."

Nina left the hospital the same way she'd arrived, in a wheelchair. Miguel had already installed the base in the car, and Jasmine snapped it into place, then got into the front seat, leaving Alex and Nina in the back with the baby.

"We'll need to buy clothes and go grocery shopping this week," Miguel said as he drove through the streets. "But Gabriel is taken care of."

"I'm scared to ask." Nina laughed.

"I told you, Auntie's gonna spoil that boy rotten," Jasmine shot back. "I wasn't playing."

When they turned down Riverview Drive and meandered down the windy road that ran along the St. John's River, Nina tore her eyes away from the baby for a minute to check out the beautiful scenery.

"This is nice," she said.

"Wait until you see the house," Jasmine said.

Miguel pulled up to a heavy iron gate, typing in the code and driving down the driveway. The gate closed behind them with a heavy thud. The property was similar to the one in Miami, with native trees and plants strategically planted to block people from seeing into the yard. But it was the house that caught her attention.

It was obviously a newer house, but it was built to look like an old farmhouse, with a huge porch that wrapped around the entire house, and narrow pillars spaced evenly between the rails. Miguel drove past the house, down the gravel drive that led straight to the river.

The entire property was fenced, high enough that Nina would never have to worry about Gabriel wandering to the water's edge. The gate was a lot like the one at Alex's house, which required a code to open no matter what side you were on.

"All in all, the property including the private dock is just over two acres," Miguel said. "The main house is six bedrooms, five baths, and the guest house is three and three."

"I didn't even see the guest house," Nina said. "This place is beautiful."

"It took some convincing to get them to approve this house, but it was a steal at two million, and the money that's being put in your bank account is technically from the liquidation of all Alex's legal assets. I sold them on the guest house, which makes it easier for me to keep you safe."

"You're staying here?" Nina and Jasmine said in unison.

"I'm your permanent handler. After the case was done, they asked where I wanted to go next, and this is the job I chose."

"Bold choice," Nina said, then laughed when his face went blank. "I'm just kidding. Better you than someone else. At least I know you."

"I'm not the man you think I am."

"You keep saying that, but the important parts remain."

"And what are those?"

"You've been by Alex's side for more than five years, and you've saved both our lives at one time or another. I would have gone back for Alex at the mansion if you hadn't stopped me, and I could have been shot."

Miguel pulled in front of the house and parked the car, sitting there for a moment before he killed the engine.

"We'll worry about cars and anything else later. You have enough money in the bank to live for a long time before you need to get a job. Degrees and job history have been generated for you, complete with phony references that will be verified by an agent. Basically, you just live your lives, start calling each other by your new names, and never tell anyone the truth about who you are."

Alex carried the baby carrier inside, standing behind Nina when Miguel opened the door and pushed it wide so Nina could take it all in.

"Wow," she said. "This is much better than I expected."

"It's no mansion in Miami, but it's pretty close," Miguel said.

Nina walked through the house, stopping in each of the rooms on the first floor and marveling at the size of each one. Only the living room, dining room, and nursery were furnished. Miguel had left the rest for Alex and Nina to put their stamp on, just making sure that they would have some creature comforts while they got settled.

There were two bedrooms downstairs with a bathroom between them. They were empty, as were three of the four rooms on the second floor.

"I know that having dinner together is important to you," Miguel said. "So, I picked out this large farm table so no matter what we're all doing, we always have a place to meet for dinner."

"Thank you," Nina said. "I still think about those nights and miss the faces around that table."

"They were thugs," Jasmine said.

"They were, but they were people, too, and they were all very kind to me. In fact, the only person who wasn't nice to me was Miguel. Apparently, he thought his salty attitude was going to run me off."

Miguel laughed.

"You can't say that I didn't try."

"And fail."

When the laughter died down, Nina changed the subject. "What are we going to do about the rest of the rooms? I just had a baby, there's no way I'm sleeping on the couch or the floor."

"Alex and I can finish shopping for furniture today while you and Tiana figure out what we need for the kitchen and toiletries. When you feel better, there's a mall about twenty minutes away with plenty of high-end clothing stores. There's a purse on the kitchen table with your new IDs, credit cards, and SIM cards for your phones. There's also a business card for the local grocery delivery service. Figure out what you want to stock the kitchen with, and use that card. It has a high limit, so don't worry about a budget."

"They deliver groceries here?" Jasmine said.

"They deliver everything here," Nina said. "For the right price."

"Before we leave," Alex said, "I want to see the nursery."

He grabbed the car seat by the handle, careful not to wake the baby sleeping inside. Nina followed him up the stairs while Jasmine and Miguel stayed downstairs. When she turned down the hall and saw what Jasmine had done, she gasped.

"It's beautiful," she called down, stopping herself from calling her "Jazzy" just in time, then turning back to the room. "It's so beautiful."

The windows were open wide, the little room at the end of the hall with windows on two sides. Despite the fresh, dove gray paint, the room smelled fresh. The furniture was white, the bedding and fabric on the rocking glider pale yellow. Bright blue pillows adorned the recliner and the glider, and on the one wall without a door or a window, Jasmine had painted a giant mural, complete with ocean animals beneath the dark blue waters of the sea, and dolphins jumping into the sky-blue air.

Alex set Gabriel down in his carrier, wrapping his arms around her waist and holding her as they both looked out the east window to the river beyond.

"This view is amazing," she said, testing out the rocker, which faced east. "I want this room for myself."

"I didn't know Jasmine could paint."

"She has a lot of talents. She just needs focus."

"She'll find that here. She can paint until her heart's content. None of us have to work, despite what Jaime, I mean Miguel, thinks."

"What do you think he's going to say when he finds out you have access to your offshore accounts?"

"It doesn't matter. By the time it comes up, it will be awhile down the road. He never has to find out. As soon as we have our own cars and he loosens his hold a little, I'm going to close the accounts the DEA opened for us and move our money to another bank."

"Or you can leave those accounts and use them for some small, recurring payment."

"That's why you're the brains of this family," he said. "So, yes. We can open an account at another bank now that we're married and all that."

"I thought that was a nice touch."

"So did I. If you want to have a big wedding, we can."

"Everyone I would invite is already here."

"Me too."

"Oh Alex, I think the hardest part of this is calling you Vance. And what will we tell Gabriel when he's older?"

"We'll tell him the truth. Everyone has a past, and ours is just a little more exciting. It's best if he never finds out the whole truth."

"I know."

"Don't worry about those things now. We have our whole lives ahead of us, and because of the big mouth of Carlos's stupid lawyer, Jasmine is here, too."

"After all we've been through, I still feel so lucky. I have the perfect family, and my best friend is here with us. This house is amazing, and I can't think of a man I'd rather spend the rest of this crazy life with than you."

"It worked out better than I could have hoped."

Gabriel fussed from his carrier, and Alex went to him, unbuckling him while Nina sat in the glider, then handing him off for a feeding. He leaned against the wall, watching Nina with a sweet expression on his face.

"What?"

"You. Motherhood looks beautiful on you."

"I can't believe everything that's happened since I met you. It's like a dream. A crazy, perfectly imperfect dream."

She rocked Gabriel until he finished eating, then Alex took him to burp him before carefully laying him in the bassinet beside the glider.

"Don't worry, we'll have this place feeling like home in no time. Miguel and I will be back in a few hours, and by tonight, you'll be sleeping on a luxury mattress in our room with Gabriel in the bassinet beside you."

"Anything is going to feel like luxury after that safehouse," she quipped, then fell silent, looking at the window before she spoke again. "Do you think you can learn to love this house as much as you loved the last one?"

"Of course, I can," he said, kissing her cheek and reaching into the bassinet to stroke Gabriel's cheek as he drifted off to sleep again. "It's not the house that I loved. It's who's inside it that makes a house a home."

THANKS FOR READING!

This book is part of a bestselling series called "United States Of Billionaires". Every book features a different billionaire in a different city and very soon we could be coming to your home town!

Below are all the books currently available, **is a city you love in there?** Download now and check it out. (*Be warned, all these books are extra STEAMY!*)

Book 1 – The Billionaire From San Diego
Book 2 – The Billionaire From Atlanta
Book 3 – The Billionaire From Dallas
Book 4 – The Billionaire From New York City

Book 5 – The Billionaire From San Francisco

Book 6 – The Billionaire From Chicago
Book 7 – The Billionaire From Miami
Book 8 – The Billionaire From Hawaii

Collect the whole series!

Peace, love and high heels!

Lena & The Simply BWWM Team

Fancy A FREE BWWM Romance Book??

Join the "**Romance Recommended**" Mailing list today and gain access to an exclusive **FREE** classic BWWM Romance book along with many others more to come. You will also be kept up to date on the best book deals in the future on the hottest new BWWM Romances.

* **Get FREE Romance Books For Your Kindle & Other Cool giveaways**

* **Discover Exclusive Deals & Discounts Before Anyone Else!**

* **Be The FIRST To Know about Hot New Releases From Your Favorite Authors**

Click The Link Below To Access This Now!

__Oh Yes! Sign Me Up To Romance Recommended For FREE!__

Already subscribed?

OK, Read On!

A MUST HAVE!

BABY SHOWER

10 BOOK PREGNANCY ROMANCE BOXSET

50% DISCOUNT!!

An amazing chance to own 10 complete books for one LOW price!

This package features some of the biggest selling authors from the world of Pregnancy Romance. They have collaborated to bring you this super-sized portion of love, sex and romance involving the drama of a baby on the way!

1 - Tasha Blue – The Best Man's Baby
2 - Alexis Gold – The Movie Star's Designer Baby
3 - Cherry Kay – The Tycoon's Convenient Baby
4 - CJ Howard – The Billionaire's Love Child
5 - Kimmy Love – Her Bosses Baby?
6 - Lacey Legend – The Billionaire's Unwanted Baby
7 - Lena Skye – A Baby Of Convenience
8 - Monica Castle – The Cowboy's Secret Baby
9 - Tasha Blue – Fireman's Baby
10 -Alexis Gold – The Billionaire's Secret Baby

TAP HERE TO DOWNLOAD NOW!

ANOTHER MUST HAVE!

TALL, WHITE & ALPHA

10 BILLIONAIRE ROMANCE BOOKS BOXSET

50% DISCOUNT!!

An amazing chance to own 10 complete books for one LOW price!

This package features some of the biggest selling authors from the world of Billionaire Romance. They have collaborated to bring you this super-sized portion of love, sex and romance involving loveable heroines and Tall, White and Alpha Billionaire men.

1 The Billionaire's Designer Bride – Alexis Gold
2 The Prettiest Woman – Lena Skye
3 How To Marry A Billionaire – Susan Westwood
4 Seduced By The Italian Billionaire – CJ Howard
5 The Cowboy Billionaire's Proposal – Monica Castle
6 Seduced By The Secret Billionaire – Cherry Kay
7 Billionaire Impossible – Lacey Legend
8 Matched With The British Billionaire – Kimmy Love

9 The Billionaire's Baby Mama – Tasha Blue
10 The Billionaire's Arranged Marriage – CJ Howard

TAP HERE TO DOWNLOAD THIS NOW!

Made in the USA
Coppell, TX
03 June 2025